SO FAR AWAY

"You'll be the first married camp counselor at Camp Mohawk," Meg said.

Julie smiled a little sadly. "Oh, Meg," she said. "I'll really miss Camp Mohawk and all you girls."

"What do you mean 'miss us'?" Laura asked.

Stevie knew exactly what Julie meant. "She means she won't be coming back to Camp Mohawk this summer, don't you, Julie?" Stevie swallowed hard and looked up at the girl who was like a big sister to her. She hoped Julie wasn't going to say she was right.

"Well, I'll certainly come to visit, Stevie," said Julie a little wistfully. "But, you know, Eric goes to school in New Hampshire."

"That's so far away from here," Stevie said.

P.S. We'll Miss You
Yours 'Til the Meatball Bounces
2 Sweet 2 B 4-Gotten
Remember Me, When This You See
Sealed with a Hug
Friends 'Til the Ocean Waves
Friends 4-Ever Minus 1
Mysteriously Yours
C U When the Snow Falls
Yours 'Til the Wedding Rings

YOURS 'TIL THE WEDDING RINGS

Deirdre Corey

AN
APPLE
PAPERBACK

SCHOLASTIC INC.
New York Toronto London Auckland Sydney

ISBN 0-590- 45110-3

12 11 10 9 8 7 6 5 4   3 4 5 6 7/9

Printed in the U.S.A.   40

First Scholastic printing, January 1992

for Louise Colligan

No matter how near,
No matter how far,
Friends forever
Is what we are.

SNOW DAY

Snowflakes fell like plump puffs of powder, polka-dotting Stevie Ames's red ski cap and matching red jacket. The freckle-faced girl stopped shoveling snow off the driveway long enough to throw back her head and give up her face to the soft, lacy flakes. There was a frosty snap in the air that had turned Stevie's cheeks rosy, making the white snow stand out clearly against her skin. Where freckles weren't, snow was, so Stevie's face was decorated like some lovely valentine with red showing through here, and white there.

This was the kind of day Stevie liked best in Crispin Landing. Everything was blanketed in

1

white. Trees glistened with icicles hanging down. The sky was a snow sky, and the smell in the air told of snow even before the snow had begun falling. And the best thing about this kind of day, as far as Stevie was concerned, was that it was a school day, but school was closed because of the snow.

A posolutely absotively perfect day, thought Stevie as she stuck out her tongue to catch a couple of snowflakes. Just as she was thinking how beautifully delicate and light the flakes were, she felt a dull thump against the front of her jacket. Stevie looked down. A big, white, round spot of snow clung to her jacket where the thump had come from.

"Surprise!" sang out a familiar voice.

"Molly!" Stevie laughed. "Was that your snowball? Good shot. I thought I was the only one who could hit a target from that far away."

Molly Quindlen laughed back. "You'd be pretty hard to miss in that bright red jacket. Also, you were standing as still as a parking meter, so it was easy to zap you even from here." Before the dark-haired girl in the neon-pink and green jacket could say any more, she, too, felt a thump. "Hey!" she cried out, looking at Stevie for an explanation. "How'd you do that?"

"She didn't," came a voice from behind Molly.

Meg Milano was laughing so hard at Molly's reaction that her blonde curls bounced against the edge of her yellow-and-purple-striped stocking cap. Her gloves matched, and the snowy evidence still clung to them. "Gotcha!" giggled Meg. Then she, too, felt a thump on her purple jacket. "Ouch!"

"Oh! I didn't hurt you, did I?" said a worried voice coming up behind Meg.

Meg quickly bent down and picked up a handful of snow. She packed it into a ball and zoomed it right in Laura Ryder's direction. Laura quickly threw up her hands to protect her face, but it wasn't necessary. The snowball brushed across her long brown hair and bounced off her pale pink jacket.

Now all the girls were packing snowballs and throwing them as fast as they were made. Before long their jackets were covered, and all four of them were laughing as they tried to dodge the next snowball. Stevie held up her shovel as a shield and managed to stop a few of them. "Missed me!" she called out to Molly, just as Meg snuck up from behind and dropped a handful of snow down the back of Stevie's neck.

"Aaahhhh!" shrieked Stevie as she felt the snow melting against her warm neck. Stevie was all ready to do the same thing back to Meg, when Meg held up both hands and called out, "Truce!"

"Oh! No fair!" laughed Stevie, taking aim one last time and hurling a snowball right at Meg's upheld hands.

Meg tried to control her laughter because she had something official to say. "Listen," she began. "We have to get some work done here. Mrs. Hansen is our first customer, and we have to do a good job."

"Well, of course we'll do a good job," Stevie said definitely. "We're the Snow Busters! Crispin Landing's first all-girl snow-shoveling and snow-decorating team. When there's something white and flaky in the neighborhood, who ya gonna call? Snow Busters!"

"I love the name," Molly said, picking up one of the shovels Stevie had brought with her. "But Meg is right. We'd better get to work or else we won't get paid."

"If you two do the shoveling, and Meg and I do the decorations for the yard, we should be able to finish quickly," Laura said.

It had already been decided at their Friends 4-Ever Club meeting the day before that Stevie and Molly would shovel. Laura and Meg preferred to be the ones who made the snow figures for the yards. That had been Laura's idea.

The meeting had been held to think up ways of making money for a Valentine's Day party the next month. They didn't know exactly what they wanted to do for Valentine's Day, but they had all agreed it had to be something different and special. In past years they'd always had parties. One year, when they were much younger, they'd had a Valentine Tea Party with their dolls. Another year they'd had a luncheon. Still another year they'd had a big craft party and made valentines, decorated cookies, and made friendship bracelets, necklaces, and ankle bracelets. But this year they felt older and wanted to plan something more grown-up.

"Like what?" Stevie had groaned, fearing the worst. "Not a boy-girl party or something sick like that, I hope."

"Oh, right," Molly said. "Who would we invite? Willy and Simon, those pains-in-the-neck? Or your brother Mike and some of his creepy friends?"

"That's what I mean," Stevie agreed. "I hope we're not thinking like that yet."

"No," Meg assured both Stevie and Molly. "I didn't mean that, although Valentine's Day is the day when Cupid's arrows go flying around — and if you're hit by one you fall in love."

"Don't even mention it," Stevie said. "I think one hit my mother."

"Your mother?" Laura gasped. "Stevie, what do you mean? She's in love?"

Stevie's mother had been divorced since Stevie was two years old. Mrs. Ames had spent most of her time adjusting to life as a single mother, getting a career going in real estate, and taking classes at night to get another degree. Dating had been the farthest thing from her mind. Until recently.

"I don't know if she's in love. But she's definitely in like, and I definitely *don't* like it. She walks around singing all the time, even early in the morning! It's weird."

That was all Stevie had said about it, and the other girls could see that Stevie wasn't in the mood to talk about it anymore then. In fact, Stevie changed the subject herself and came up with the idea of shoveling snow for money. Laura added her idea for creating lawn sculptures out of snow. "Not just ordinary snowmen," she'd said, "but snow cats, snow ladies, snow anything. We can charge by the sculpture."

Before the meeting was over they called Stevie's good friend Mrs. Hansen, to ask if she'd like her driveway shoveled and her lawn decorated.

The grandmotherly woman was delighted with both ideas and had told them to come over the next morning. And here they were, shovels in hand. As the girls got to work, Stevie laughed and said to her friends, "We won't charge Mrs. Hansen for the snowball fight."

"Oh, but you should!" came Mrs. Hansen's voice from the front doorway. "I can't remember the last time I enjoyed watching anything so much. You girls certainly know how to have fun."

"Hi, Mrs. Hansen!" Stevie called out first.

"We're just getting to work now," Meg added. "Don't worry about a thing."

"I'm not worried at all," said the gray-haired woman whose cheeks were as rosy as Stevie's. "I know you girls will do a wonderful job. It's not every day a person can get the driveway shoveled and lawn decorations at the same time. It's a wonderful idea!"

"Snow Busters at your service!" Molly added happily.

"And Snow Builders," Laura said, looking around for the perfect spot to build the snow sculptures.

"Well, you girls enjoy the snow. More coming, so they say. Looks like you'll have plenty of business if this keeps up." Mrs. Hansen looked at the sky and saw the gray clouds dropping just a light dusting of flakes.

"And we'll have plenty of time to do it because school will be closed again," said Molly.

"I'll check on you in a while and see how you're doing," Mrs. Hansen said before she shut the door. "Just ring the bell if you need anything."

The girls got right to work without stopping to play anymore. Stevie and Molly were a perfect shoveling team. They went from one side of the driveway to the other, making two perfectly cleared paths as they pushed their shovels in front of them. After shoveling the driveway, Stevie and Molly cleared the walkway and the front steps. When they were completely finished, they heard Meg and Laura giggling from where they were working under the icicle-covered tree.

"What's so funny?" Stevie asked, trying to see around them. Both Laura and Meg were standing in front of whatever they had made and were looking over their work.

"Let us see," Molly called over to them. "Stand back."

Meg and Laura stepped back and each held out a hand toward the two figures they had made. "Presenting the Greatest Snow Couple on

Earth!" Meg said in her most official voice.

"The bride and groom, Mr. and Mrs. Snow!" Laura heralded.

Molly immediately went running over to get a closer look. She saw the two snow people and gasped. "They look so real!" she said. "The girl looks so pretty and the groom looks so handsome!"

The snow bride and groom were not like any snowmen any of the girls had ever made or seen before. Instead of round ball bodies and big round ball heads, this pair was tall and shaped like a real bride and groom. The bride's face had a delicate nose, perfectly heart-shaped lips, hair to her shoulders, and a long veil flowing down the back of her snow-white dress. Her dress had a bell-shaped skirt, and in her carefully sculpted hands she held a bouquet of white flowers. The groom stood taller than the bride. His long, straight legs were topped by a waistcoat that had long, formal tails. On his lapel was a snow flower that matched his bride's bouquet. His jaw was square and his nose straight. They were a perfect couple.

Stevie couldn't take it too seriously. As the others admired the details on the faces and clothes, she picked up her shovel, held it upside down like a bouquet of flowers, and began the wedding march down a lumpy aisle of piled-up snow. She screeched, "Here comes the bride, the groom better hide," and tripped clumsily all along the way.

Meg, Molly, and Laura laughed until tears rolled down their cheeks. The harder they laughed, the more Stevie carried on with tipsy curtsies and an exaggerated fluttering of her eyelashes. She pretended to blush; she pretended to get tangled in her veil. Then suddenly she stopped, threw down the shovel bouquet, and turned so her back was to the girls. She threw her arms around herself so that from the back it looked as if someone else were hugging her. A loud smacking sound of kissing punctuated her breathless declarations of eternal love, "for better or for worse — probably for worse."

Now Mrs. Hansen's laughter joined the others' as she appeared on the freshly shoveled doorstep with a plateful of warm, heart-shaped cookies, and mugs full of steaming hot cocoa. "Oh, Stevie!" she laughed, trying to keep the tray steady in her hands. "You make a most unusual bride!"

"That's about as close to being a bride as you'll ever see me," Stevie said, stabbing her shovel into a snowbank and holding the handle firmly. "There's no bride like a snow bride!"

"Well, in this case that's definitely true," agreed Mrs. Hansen. "This snow bride and groom are the loveliest I've ever seen. And my driveway looks as clear as in summer. You girls have done a wonderful job."

"Thank you, Mrs. Hansen," they all said together, coming forward to have some cocoa and a cookie.

"And thanks for the winter picnic, too!" added Meg.

"Heart-shaped cookies," said Laura admiringly as she picked one up off the tray. "The perfect treat for a snow wedding!"

Mrs. Hansen put the tray down on the step and went inside to get the money for the Snow Busters-Snow Builders. As soon as she had disappeared, a small, red car pulled into the driveway and the horn beeped cheerily. "It's Julie!" Stevie cried excitedly. "Hey, Julie! Hi!" Stevie was the first to leave the snacks and run to greet the tall, reddish-blonde-haired girl who was getting out of the car. It was Julie McCarthy, all the girls' favorite counselor from Camp Mohawk. Julie was a college student from Minnesota attending Camden College for Women not too far from Crispin Landing. She rented a room from Mrs. Hansen and drove back and forth to classes every day. All the girls loved her, but Stevie liked to think she was Julie's favorite. At camp, Julie always spent extra time coaching Stevie in hockey and softball. And it was Stevie who got Mrs. Hansen and Julie together when Julie was looking for a room and Mrs. Hansen was looking for a renter.

"Stevie!" Julie said, throwing her arms around the snow-covered girl. "You look like you've been buried in this stuff! Are you freezing?"

"Nope," replied Stevie. "We've been working too hard to get cold. Molly and I have been shoveling, and Meg and Laura have been — "

"Let me see," Julie said, turning her attention to the snow figures. She took her arm off Stevie's shoulders and stepped through the deep snow to get a closer look. "Oh, you guys!" she exclaimed. "I can't believe you made them by yourselves! They're beautiful! They look frozen in a state of happiness. Winter weddings are definitely beautiful, aren't they?"

"I thought everyone gets married in June," Stevie said, walking over to stand by Julie again. "Everyone who does get married, I mean."

A big smile spread across Julie's face. "Well, not everyone gets married in June," Julie said. "Take me, for example." As she spoke she removed her bright blue glove from her left hand.

Meg saw the diamond ring first. "Julie!" she cried. "Where'd you get the ring? Does this mean you're getting married?"

"Are you?" Laura asked, too.

"When?" Molly added. "Really, are you?"

Now the girls rushed forward to look at Julie's outstretched hand. On the ring finger of her left hand was a small, sparkling diamond engagement ring. Julie tried to answer all the questions the girls were asking. "Yes, I am getting married," she began. "Eric and I decided we'd get married right after my graduation. Then we can be together while he finishes graduate school."

"Hold on a minute," Stevie interrupted. "But you already graduated last month."

"Yes, Stevie," said Julie. She pulled Stevie closer to her and shared her exciting news. "Eric and I are getting married next month! On Valentine's Day!"

"Valentine's Day," bubbled Molly.

"Next month!" Meg repeated, clapping her gloved hands together excitedly.

"What a perfect day for a wedding," Laura added, looking over at her snow bride and trying to picture Julie in its place.

Julie continued. "And here's the best news of all," she said, looking just about ready to burst with the next surprise. "I want all of you to be my junior bridesmaids! You'll all be in the wedding!"

"Junior bridesmaids!" Meg and Molly exclaimed together.

"All of us?" Laura asked, hardly able to believe the good luck.

"All of you," Julie laughed. "Of course, all of you. I wouldn't have the most important event of my life without my most important campers there to be a part of it, would I?"

The next few minutes seemed like a movie to Stevie, only she was not in it. She stood as frozen as the bride and groom and watched as her friends hugged Julie, sputtered words of excitement, and gushed with happiness. They all wanted to know everything. Where would the wedding be? Would it be a small wedding or a big one? Who else was coming? The questions flew at Julie, and all she could do was laugh as she tried to answer them. But Stevie said nothing. Her mouth opened to say something, anything, but no words came out. She stepped out of the circle of excited girls and tried to hear what Julie was saying, but her own thoughts drowned out the sound of Julie's voice.

Julie's getting married, Stevie kept thinking to herself. *She's really getting married.*

Mrs. Hansen's voice interrupted Stevie's thoughts. "What's all the excitement out here?" she called from the steps. "Oh, Julie! Hello, dear. Did you just get home?"

"Yes," Meg answered for Julie. "And she has the biggest surprise ever. Julie's getting married!"

"On Valentine's Day!" Laura added.

"And we're all going to be in the wedding!" Molly shouted out with glee.

The cold air was warmed by the laughter and excited chatter that filled it. All the talk was about Julie's wedding and about the part the girls would play in it. It would be the first opportunity any of them had ever had to actually be a part of a wedding. All Meg, Molly, and Laura could talk about was what they would be wearing and how beautiful they would all look.

Stevie just listened, but tried not to hear what she was hearing. She couldn't explain, even to herself, the feeling that had come over her. She felt something wet landing on her cheeks. She looked up at the sky to see if snow was starting to fall again. The clouds looked full, but snow wasn't falling yet. Stevie wiped the wetness away and realized then that it wasn't snowflakes dampening her cheeks. It was her own tears falling as silently as flakes of snow.

SISTERS FOREVER

"Oh, Stevie," said Julie when she saw that Stevie was crying. "I know you're so happy for me. That's so sweet of you." She gave Stevie another big hug. As the two stood next to each other it was easy to see why so many people had mistaken Stevie and Julie for sisters. Both had long reddish-blonde hair and blue eyes that sparkled. But what was most noticeably the same was the sprinkling of freckles across both of their noses and cheeks.

"We're *all* so happy for you, Julie," Molly cried with delight. "Everyone at camp always thought you and Eric were the perfect couple."

"And they were right," Meg added. "And

you'll be the first married camp counselor at Camp Mohawk."

Julie smiled a little sadly. "Oh, Meg," she said. "I'll really miss Camp Mohawk and all you girls."

"What do you mean 'miss us'?" Laura asked.

Stevie knew exactly what Julie meant. "She means she won't be coming back to Camp Mohawk this summer, don't you, Julie?" Stevie swallowed hard and looked up at the girl who was like a big sister to her. She hoped Julie wasn't going to say she was right.

"Well, I'll certainly come to visit, Stevie," said Julie a little wistfully. "But, you know, Eric goes to school in New Hampshire."

"That's so far away from here," Stevie almost whispered as the truth began to sink in. *Julie's getting married. Julie is going to be with Eric. Julie is not going to live in Crispin Landing anymore. Julie is not going to be at Camp Mohawk anymore. Julie is not going to be with me anymore!*

"Eric and I will drive over here sometimes, I'm sure," Julie assured Stevie. "Maybe during his semester break we'll visit. Eric and I will be fixing up an apartment and that will keep us busy for a while, but you know Eric and I will want to come by the camp and see all our friends."

Eric and I. Eric and I. Eric and I. That was all Stevie could hear. It almost seemed to her that Julie was already off with Eric, leaving her and the other girls behind.

"Oh, Julie, dear," said Mrs. Hansen happily. "This is such happy news, but I will certainly miss you in my house. It's been such a perfect arrangement — you're like a granddaughter to me."

Julie hugged Mrs. Hansen. "Oh, you know I'll miss you so much, too, but I'll write and I'll call and I hope you'll come to visit — "

"Eric and I," finished Stevie for Julie.

"Eric and *me*." Julie laughed as she ruffled Stevie's hair, which hung out from under the red cap.

"Whatever," said Stevie gloomily.

"Of course we'll come and visit you," bubbled Meg. "We can take a bus all together or our parents could drive us."

"Where there's a will there's a way," said Molly positively.

"Where there's a will there's a funeral," Stevie said. Everybody laughed at her joke, but Stevie didn't even smile.

"Why don't you all come inside and we'll celebrate," said Mrs. Hansen. "I've got plenty more of those cookies and lots of hot chocolate."

The girls accepted the invitation immediately. All of them loved Mrs. Hansen's house. It was always filled with delicious smells of freshly baked goodies, and everything in each room had an interesting story to go with it. Mrs. Hansen had traveled a lot with her husband before he died. Tables were filled with souvenirs from countries around the world. And the nicest thing about Mrs. Hansen was that she encouraged the girls to touch everything, even her most fragile glass figures from Venice.

Stevie remembered the first time she had brought Julie over to Mrs. Hansen's house. Julie had put up a notice on the camp bulletin board advertising that she needed a room to rent. Mrs. Hansen had put up a notice at the grocery store advertising that she had a room to rent. Stevie knew the match would be perfect, and she was right. When Stevie introduced Julie to Mrs. Hansen, they liked each other right away. One of their first conversations had been about the glass figures on the end table.

"I see you've been to Venice," Julie had said when she saw the tiny glass sculptures. She bent down to look closely at a small figure of a bride sitting in a heart-shaped chair. "I was there last spring with my school choral group. I saw figures like these when I was there, but we were

19

so busy with our singing engagements, we didn't have time to buy souvenirs."

"Oh, my," Mrs. Hansen had said. "I always like to have something to remind me of places and people that are special to me." She looked around at all the knick-knacks and unusual items on the shelves and mantle and tables. "I guess I found something special in a lot of places."

The arrangements had been made that very afternoon. Julie would move her things in the next day. That had been almost six months ago, and things had been happy ever since.

"Just pile your jackets on the chair by the door," Mrs. Hansen told all her visitors. "We'll sit in the living room by the fireplace and, Julie, you can tell us all about your plans. Valentine's Day is not very far away."

The girls settled down in front of the warm fire. Julie sat in a flowered wing chair, and Stevie sat on the floor at her feet. Julie reached out a hand and smoothed Stevie's straggly hair. "One of these days, Stephanie Ames," she said in a mock stern tone, "we're going to have to fix this hair of yours."

"You'll *have* to fix it for the wedding," Meg said. "Especially when you're a bridesmaid!"

Stevie flipped up her hair and piled half of it

on top of her head. "How's this?" she said. "Am I too, too gorgeous?"

"You'll all look too, too gorgeous in your bridesmaids' dresses," Julie said. "And Eric and I want you girls to pick them out yourselves."

At the words "Eric and I," Stevie tuned out. She stared into the fireplace for a minute, then switched her glance over to the table of glass figures. There was a sailboat, a unicorn, a mermaid on a crystal rock, a gondola, a bird in a nest, a small girl holding a bouquet of flowers, and the figure of the bride sitting in the heart-shaped chair. For no reason at all, Stevie went over to the figures and moved the little girl with the bouquet closer to the bigger girl in the heart-shaped chair. Then she went back to her place at Julie's feet. None of the others noticed what Stevie had done. They were all too interested in Julie's wedding plans.

"And of course, Eric and I want you all to come to the rehearsal dinner," she was saying when Stevie tuned back in to the conversation. "The wedding will be at the church on Fairfield Street, then the reception will be at the Old Crispin Inn. It will be a small family wedding with Eric's and my closest friends, but of course the guest list keeps growing every time Eric and I check it over again. So I think it's going to be bigger than we thought."

Laura could not stop thinking about what it would feel like to wear a beautiful dress and walk down the aisle in front of the bridesmaids and the bride.

Meg could only think of all the fun of making all the plans. "I'll organize the shopping trip to pick out dresses!" she said excitedly. "Won't it be fun to all shop together?"

"We can make a big day of it," Molly said enthusiastically. "We can plan to have lunch at the Yellow Brick Road restaurant."

"Will you meet us there, Julie?" Laura asked.

"I'll have to see what day it is that you're doing that," Julie replied. "There are so many arrangements that have to be made. I don't know how I'll get it all done. My mother told me it would be hard to plan a wedding so far from home, but Eric and I wanted to have it here because all our friends are closer to here than to my parents' home in Minnesota."

"And also, then *we* can be junior bridesmaids!" added Molly.

Things were so cozy at Mrs. Hansen's house that the girls hardly noticed the time passing. Julie ran up to her room and brought down stacks of bridal magazines and catalogs of dresses, floral arrangements, and travel brochures. Over lunch they talked about Julie's wedding dress. The girls poured over the magazines "oohing" and "aahhing" at every picture of every bride walking down every aisle.

The junior bridesmaids took turns pretending to throw rose petals along the make-believe aisle as Julie practiced slowly walking to the wedding music that Laura, Meg, and Molly tried to sing in harmony. While her friends played wedding, Stevie pretended to be more interested in the magazines. She kept her head down and tried to imagine that the brides in the pictures had nothing to do with her Julie.

As the afternoon wore on, Mrs. Hansen treated the girls to popcorn and apple cider while they all talked about Julie and Eric's honeymoon plans. "Eric and I decided Bermuda would be nice. We'll take a cruise on a ship to get there, then we'll fly back to New Hampshire," Julie explained.

When Stevie heard "New Hampshire" again, she didn't want to hear any more. She stood up and looked out the window at the darkening sky. Clouds heavy with snow formed overhead, and the ice-covered trees looked cold and bare. Stevie saw the snow bride and groom standing together under the biggest tree. The cold didn't seem to bother them a bit.

Molly came over to stand next to Stevie and gasped when she saw how dark it was getting. "Ohmigosh!" she said. "We've been talking all day! Don't you think we'd better go?"

"Oh, I could do this for weeks," Laura sighed. "It's so much fun planning everything and looking at all the dresses."

Julie smiled. "Oh, girls," she said warmly, "this *has* been fun. You really are the greatest girls in the world, and I know you'll make the greatest junior bridesmaids, too."

The girls gathered around Julie to give her hugs before they left the cozy setting in Mrs. Hansen's living room. When it was Stevie's turn for a hug, Julie held her for an extra second and then stepped back and looked her right in the eye. "Friends forever, right, Stevie?" whispered Julie.

Stevie looked up at Julie and thought for a second. "No," she said softly. "Sisters forever."

TOO BAD, TOO SAD

"Turning to our school closings now," said the morning newsman. "Due to heavy snows, all Camden schools will be closed again today. I repeat, all Camden schools will be closed again today."

"Yippee!" said Stevie, flipping the switch to turn off the television. It was only 6:30 A.M., but she had crept downstairs to watch the early morning news so she'd be the first to get the official word that school was closed. Soon after, the phone started ringing.

"Did you hear?" Molly's sleepy voice asked. "No school."

"Yeah," Stevie said excitedly. "And did you

look out yet? I can't believe how deep it is out there!"

"And still falling. What do you want to do today?" Molly yawned as she spoke.

"Well, I guess the first thing to do is wait for the rest of the world to wake up," Stevie laughed.

"The rest of the world *is* up," Molly said. "Meg called me after Laura called her."

"You're right," agreed Stevie. "The rest of the world *is* up then. What did Meg say?"

"She wants to have a club meeting at her house first thing," Molly told Stevie.

"Fine with me. So we'll bring our snow shovels?" Stevie was already planning the day's money-making in her mind.

"Well, no," Molly said. "No shovels. It's not going to be that kind of meeting."

"What? This is the biggest snowstorm we've had in centuries! We've gotta get out there and dig for dollars!" Stevie didn't understand why Meg would want to have a meeting about anything except how much to charge for shoveling snow this deep. "Well, what is the meeting about then?"

"Dresses," Molly said, almost timidly.

"Dresses?" said Stevie with surprise.

"Dresses," repeated Molly.

Stevie lost her quiet morning voice and spoke loudly enough to cause her brother Dave to call out, "Pipe down, Stevie! We're trying to sleep up here!"

"What do you mean dresses? We have to have a meeting about dresses? For what? Are we going to start wearing uniforms for the Snow Busters or something? What kind of dresses? Snow dresses?" Stevie tried to regain control of her voice, but she couldn't understand why her friends wanted to have a club meeting about something she had no interest in at all.

"Not snow dresses," laughed Molly. "Wedding dresses."

The word "wedding" was a stinging reminder of the pain Stevie had felt the day before. She had been surprised by her own tears. As Stevie and the girls walked home from Mrs. Hansen's house, Meg, Molly, and Laura were full of talk about being junior bridesmaids, about how beautiful Julie would look in a wedding dress, and even about how cute Eric was! Stevie was just full of sadness.

"We're not going to waste a snow day meeting on wedding dresses, I hope!" Stevie sputtered now to Molly, who held the phone out from her ear a little because Stevie's voice level was rising again.

27

Molly was quick to defend Meg and the meeting. "No, no," she said. "I'm sure we're going to talk about a lot of things. We always do, you know."

Stevie felt the same strange feeling she'd felt yesterday. There seemed to be knots all through her, in her stomach, in her throat, even in her head. She felt tears coming back to her eyes even though the newsman had just given her the happiest news. A big teardrop rolled across her freckles. Stevie could not believe she was really crying again, and over something so totally silly and ridiculous as her camp counselor getting married. Julie was her counselor, her coach, her swimming instructor, her friend. That was all. It wasn't like Julie was her mother or something!

"Get a grip, Stevarino," Stevie said out loud, forgetting that Molly was on the other end of the phone line listening.

"What?" Molly asked. "Get a grip on what? Wedding dresses?"

"No, never mind," Stevie said, forcing her tears to stop. "So when is this meeting about all these dresses?"

"Not 'all these dresses,' " Molly corrected laughingly. "*A* dress. *A* dress."

"Gettysburg *a* dress or your home *a* dress?" Stevie joked.

"The junior bridesmaid dress that we're all going to wear," Molly said, clicking her tongue against the roof of her mouth.

"We're all wearing *one* dress?" Stevie joked some more.

"Funny," Molly said, clicking her tongue again. "You know what I mean. We'll all be wearing the same style, the same color. That's what I mean. Not that we'll all be wearing the same *one* dress. Uh! Stevie Ames, sometimes you are impossible!"

Stevie knew Molly didn't really mean what she said. Molly was Stevie's closest friend. Stevie knew one of the things Molly liked best about her was the way she always made a joke out of everything. That was what everybody liked about Stevie, but Molly knew Stevie best. They'd spent many hours sitting on Molly's bed, making up stories about the little pink houses on Molly's wallpaper. And as they made up wallpaper stories, they talked about other things, too. Sometimes the subject was problems with brothers — Stevie's problems with her brothers Dave and Mike, and Molly's problems with her little brother, Scotty. Other times they talked about school — which teachers were nice, which ones were mean. Still other times they talked about parents and their rules. There were no secrets

29

between Stevie and Molly. They knew everything there was to know about each other. One thing Molly knew about Stevie was that her jokes were sometimes the hiding places for other thoughts that were bothering her. But this time, Molly didn't know what was on Stevie's mind. Even Stevie herself was not certain.

"Well, anyway," Stevie continued their conversation, "so what time are we meeting?"

"Meg said nine. Is that okay with you?" Molly asked.

"Nine is okay with me, but I'm not so sure the meeting will be." Before Molly could say anything, Stevie quickly finished with, "I'm bringing my shovel anyway. After all, we can't possibly talk about dresses the *whole* time."

Stevie was wrong. They could talk about dresses the whole time, and they did.

"I now declare this Friends 4-Ever Club meeting officially started," said Meg in her club meeting voice. She pounded a small hammer down on the pile of her special club stationery with the kittens across the top. The girls stopped their chattering at the sound of the hammer's thud. "The first order of business," continued Meg, "is the business of what we are all going to wear as junior bridesmaids for Julie's wedding."

Stevie rolled her eyes and flopped back against Meg's bed. Meg's fat, orange cat, Marmalade, was startled out of a catnap and stretched his paws so they reached Stevie's hair. His claws pulled her hair a little bit, but Stevie didn't care. She reached one hand back over her head and patted the furball on the bed. Marmalade leaped over Stevie's head and went running under the bed.

"See," said Stevie. "I guess I'm not the only one who doesn't want to sit around talking about dresses." She slumped down lower on the floor, crossed her arms over her chest, and pouted.

Meg and Laura didn't seem to notice. Molly looked over at Stevie and wondered why her friend was getting so upset over nothing.

"Julie said we can decide the color of the dresses ourselves," Meg continued. "She said the regular bridesmaids are wearing red velvet. We can choose red velvet too, or pink."

"Ooo," Laura said. "Won't Julie look so beautiful in her white wedding dress with all the bridesmaids in red velvet behind her? She'll be the most beautiful bride ever to walk down the aisle."

"Down the aisle and out of our lives completely," Stevie added.

"She'll be Mrs. Eric T. Bowen," Molly beamed.

"She'll be Mrs. Eric T. Gone-for-Good," Stevie joked.

"Hey," said Meg. "We're talking about a wedding, not a funeral, you know."

"It's not like we'll never see her again," Laura said softly.

"Of course we'll see her," Molly said. "She'll come back to visit all the time."

"She'll change," said Stevie solemnly.

"Weddings don't change people," Meg said, sounding as though she'd done some kind of study on the subject.

"A wedding is changing all of you," Stevie said, standing up and grabbing her red jacket. Her face was turning red, too. "Well, it is changing you!" she said too loudly. "Yesterday we were all outside being Snow Busters and Snow Builders and trying to make money for our club! As soon as everyone finds out about being in the wedding it doesn't seem to matter at all that this is the best snow we'll ever have! Nobody even cares about those plans anymore. That's what I mean. And after Julie's married she won't care about us anymore, either!"

Stevie threw open Meg's bedroom door and ran down the stairs and out the front door. She picked up her snow shovel, which she'd leaned up against Meg's house, and started walking home. Pushing the shovel in front of her, she made a path on the sidewalk as she went. Snow was still falling, and Stevie noticed that the angels she'd made in the snow on her way over to Meg's earlier were already filled in.

Even the cold air didn't cool down Stevie after her outburst at the meeting. She turned and looked back at Meg's house. Three faces were pressed against the window in Meg's bedroom. Stevie turned back around, hoping none of them had seen her looking. Of course they had, and three voices talked all at once wondering what had gotten into Stevie.

"What did I say?" Meg asked.

"Is she mad?" Laura worried.

"Where's she going?" Molly wondered.

"Home, I think," answered Meg.

Molly wanted to go after Stevie, but Meg and Laura had started talking about the wedding again and were discussing the advantages of red over pink.

Stevie didn't know what her three friends were discussing, and for the moment she didn't really care. Even a snow day and no school couldn't cheer Stevie up. For a minute she considered ringing a doorbell to ask if the people wanted her to shovel their driveway, but with the snow falling as hard as it was, she was pretty sure everyone would want to wait. Instead, Stevie kept going until she was at the corner of her street, Half Moon Lane.

"Oh, no," Stevie said, kicking her shovel for emphasis. "Him again!"

The "him" was Bob. Not "Mr. Reston," like they used to call him, but "Bob." Stevie recognized the blue car parked in front of her house as the one belonging to the man with whom Stevie's mother had already had two Saturday night dates.

"What's *he* doing here on a Wednesday morning?" Stevie said out loud. Then she realized that Bob probably had a day off from school, too, because of the snow. He taught English Literature at the college where Molly's father taught.

Before Stevie got all the way up to her house the front door opened and out came her mother and Bob. Stevie couldn't believe what she was seeing. Her mother didn't even look like her usual self! Both she and the tall man with glasses next to her were dressed in ski clothes. But Stevie's mother's hair was in two ponytails, and she wore a ski headband around her head. She was holding onto Bob's arm and laughing in a way Stevie had never heard her laugh before.

"Oh, Bob," said Stevie's mother, "the snow's so deep!"

" 'The snow's so deep!' " Stevie mimicked to herself in a too-cute voice. She felt sick. She didn't want to go home now. Molly lived only two houses up the street, but Molly was at Meg's, and Stevie didn't want to go back there.

"Oh, Bob," Stevie heard her mother saying again. "Are the roads going to be clear enough to drive on?"

"Well, he drove here, didn't he?" Stevie murmured.

"Well, I drove here now, didn't I, Judy?" Bob laughed.

Stevie just rolled her eyes and decided the only thing to do was go home, even if it meant she had to stop and say "hi" to Bob. Just as she was figuring out how to say it in a way that didn't sound friendly, but at the same time didn't sound rude, Bob and her mother drove off without even noticing Stevie.

"Well, that's just great," said Stevie to no one as she trotted up her front steps. " 'Oh, Bob!' " she squeaked. " 'It's so deep!' Yeecch!"

"What do you mean, 'Yeecch'?" said her brother Dave, who just happened to open the door as Stevie said that. "I thought you loved this stuff!"

"Don't say 'love,' " snarled Stevie. "In fact, I

35

would *love* it if I never heard the word *love* again!''

''Well, you're in a *love*ly mood, Miss Ames,'' Dave said kiddingly. ''What's the matter, Steva-rino?''

''I'll tell you what's the matter,'' Stevie said, slamming the front door closed and throwing her red ski cap down on the front hall rug. ''Everything is the matter, that's what! Julie's getting married and leaving me, my friends have left me, and now even Mom has left with *Bob*! And why do we have to call him 'Bob' now? Why can't we call him Mr. Reston like we used to?''

''Mom didn't leave,'' Dave said. ''They just went skiing over at the college.''

Stevie's brother Mike came bounding down the stairs bundled up in several layers of snow clothes. ''We have to call him 'Bob' in case they get serious. Then we won't have to change whatever we've been calling him all along.''

''Get *serious*?'' Stevie gasped in horror at the thought.

''I *am* serious,'' Mike laughed at his own joke. ''You know. Like what happened when Willy's aunt married Mr. Carrick? Willy's supposed to call him Uncle Doug now, but he still calls him

Mr. Carrick. And they've been married for almost two years!"

"And don't say 'married', either!" Stevie snapped as she headed up to her room. "I've had all I can take of all this mushy stuff."

Stevie slammed her bedroom door, and her favorite soccer poster fell off the wall. "Go ahead," Stevie yelled at the face on the curled-up poster. "You might as well leave me, too!" She threw her jacket down on the blue beanbag chair in the corner and then kicked off her snowy boots, which had already left puddles on the rug all the way up the stairs.

On her way to flop down in the chair next to her jacket, Stevie caught a glimpse of her face in the mirror. It looked different to her. The freckles were all there. Her eyes were still blue, and her hair looked just as scraggly as ever. She expected to see an angry face looking back at her. Instead she saw a worried face. Worried and a little scared. But of what? she wondered.

She sat down in the chair and twisted a piece of her hair around her finger. Next she kicked at the rug and twisted in the chair as too many thoughts turned in her mind. Under a pile of books on her night table, Stevie saw her 'N' Stuff box.

"Oh, there you are," she said to the box as she went over and pulled it out from under the books. "I was wondering where you were." Stevie's room was always full of too many things with no place to put them. She dumped the 'N' Stuff box out on her blue plaid bedspread and began searching through the treasures that lay spread out before her. She found a sparkle superball, a Clue Club membership card, a Carl Yastrzemski baseball card, stickers, pictures of Molly and her, pictures of all the Friends 4-Ever, a bell Mrs. Hansen had given her, and finally she came to the thing she was looking for.

"Julie," Stevie said in a whisper. In her hands she held a picture of Julie looking as perfect as Stevie thought she was. Her reddish-blonde hair hung down smooth and shining. Her blue eyes sparkled. Her even, white-toothed smile looked cheerful and friendly. And across her nose and cheeks were freckles, just like Stevie's.

Stevie remembered the first summer at Camp Mohawk when Julie stood at the foot of the big maple tree holding up a sign that read, BLUE JAYS. That was the name of Julie's group, and Stevie, Meg, Molly, and Laura were all in it. Right away the director of the camp had noticed that Julie and Stevie both had "sun kisses" all over their faces. The freckles that had once bothered Stevie never bothered her again after that. From that day on, Stevie felt like she'd found the big sister she didn't have at home.

Stevie turned the picture over and read what Julie had written on back:

To my little sister, Stevie —
With freckles on our faces
And sunstreaks in our hair
Don't you think we really make
A lovely-looking pair?
Have a great summer!
                              Love,
                                   Julie

Stevie turned the picture over again and stared at it another minute. Then she put everything back in the box and placed it on the shelf in her closet. Somehow, she thought, it seemed a safer place for it than under a pile of books.

The phone rang out in the hallway, and she heard Dave answer it. For a second Stevie brightened, thinking it might be for her. It wasn't. Oh, well, she thought, I didn't feel like talking anyway. But she did feel like writing. Taking out a sheet of her own special club stationery with the

blue high-top sneakers across the top, Stevie began to write:

Dear Julie,
I'm sorry I don't feel happy for you right
now. Right now I just feel

Stevie crumpled up the paper and took out a
new piece. She began another letter:

Dear Molly,
Where are you when I need you?
Yours 'til the window panes are cured,

STEVIE

When she finished her short note, Stevie
pulled on her boots and jacket, stuffed the note

in her pocket, and ran right over to Molly's house. Around in the backyard the hammock stand stood covered with snow. The hammock had been taken in for the winter, but the metal tubing still worked as a perfect place to put secret notes for Molly. Stevie was sure Molly would find the note. And then she was sure Molly would find her.

THE BETTER HALF

Stevie awoke the next morning to the sound of snowplows on the road outside of her house. It was still dark when she climbed out of bed and crept over to the window. Out front the street-lights' beams sparkled on the snow-covered lawns. Headlights high on the front of the plow trucks showed Stevie the bad news. Sand. The roads had already been plowed, and then the sand trucks had been by, too. The truck out there now wasn't even plowing. It was just checking the roads.

"Rats!" said Stevie. "School." She pulled her striped flannel nightgown around herself and shivered in the chill of the morning. The heat in the house was still on the night setting, which meant it was too early for Stevie to be out of bed. She crawled back under the covers and hoped the sand on the road was just a bad dream. When the alarm rang fifteen minutes later, Stevie knew it wasn't a dream.

"Stevie! Dave! Mike!" Mrs. Ames called through the hallway. "Time to get up. School today." Then she started singing.

Morning at the Ameses' house was a bustling time. Mrs. Ames hurried to get ready for her job at the real estate office. Mike and Dave had their usual morning argument over whose Red Sox sweatshirt was the one with the hole in it or whose socks were whose. And Stevie rushed around gathering up all her homework worksheets, books, and workbooks.

With two snow days behind her, facing the school day ahead was hard for Stevie. The other thing that was going to be hard was facing her friends. After the way she had run out of the meeting the day before, she wasn't sure what to say now. She'd waited the rest of the day and all evening for the phone to ring. She was sure Molly would call when she found the note. In fact, the phone had rung a lot, but all the calls were for someone else. When at last Stevie had turned her light out and said good night to her mother, the phone had rung again.

"Hello?" Stevie heard her mother say. "Yes, Debbie. Hi!"

Debbie. That was Molly's mother. What did she want? Stevie wondered.

"Wedding?" she heard her mother saying. "What wedding?" Pause. "No. Stevie didn't even mention it." Another longer pause. "Julie McCarthy? On Valentine's Day? That's wonderful! Why, of course Stevie can be in it. Gee, that's awfully soon, though, but I'm sure we can all get together and find dresses they'll like." Pause. "Red velvet? Oh, how lovely!"

Her mother talked a while longer and then came in to see if Stevie was still awake. She quickly closed her eyes and tried to breath like a sleeper. The last thing she wanted to talk about was the wedding!

Instead, Stevie dreamed about it. She saw Julie looking just as beautiful as Laura had said she would. Behind her were all the bridesmaids wearing beautiful red velvet dresses. Behind them came the four Friends 4-Ever. Stevie knew it was only a dream, but the dream became a nightmare at this point. First Meg, then Molly, then Laura went walking down the aisle. They were also wearing red velvet dresses and they carried small bouquets of pink, red, and white roses. The three girls kept turning around and motioning for Stevie to catch up, but in the dream Stevie couldn't move. Her dress, which was the same as the others, had somehow gotten caught on the corner of one of the church pews. The more she pulled the more she felt caught. She could see her friends calling to her, but the thing that really made her pull harder on her snagged dress was the fact that Julie was so far ahead of her. Julie was getting away from her and there wasn't anything Stevie could do about it.

"Julie!" Stevie cried out. She could hear her own voice echoing through the church. "Julie, wait! Don't go without me!" Stevie cried louder. "Julie, wait!"

"Stevie!" her mother's voice came into her ears. "Stevie, wake up, honey. Wake up. You're dreaming. It's only a dream."

Stevie felt her mother's arms around her, and suddenly the feeling of being caught went away. Now she was free to catch up with Julie, but when she opened her eyes it was not Julie sitting with her. It was her mother.

"Get a drink of water, Stevie Lou," whispered her mother in the light of the hall night-light. "Then try to go back to sleep. It was only a dream."

Stevie started to tell her mother about the dream. "It was the wedding and I — "

"Sshhh. Not now, honey. We can talk about the wedding tomorrow. Now it's time for sleeping." Her mother kissed her forehead and left Stevie alone to sleep. She almost forgot the dream and the wedding, but in the morning the wedding was the only thing on her mother's mind.

"Molly's mother called last night," said Mrs. Ames.

"Oh," said Stevie into her glass of orange juice.

"Stevie, why didn't you tell me Julie is getting married? How exciting! And you girls are going to be junior bridesmaids? Now if that isn't a dream come true I don't know what is." While she spoke, Stevie's mother buttered toast, poured cereal, handed Dave and Mike lunch money, waved them good-bye, and then gulped down a cup of coffee herself. In the hustle-bustle of the morning rush, she didn't notice that Stevie was not excited at all.

Stevie didn't say anything. What she thought to herself was, I sure hope it's *not* a dream come true! Before she could think more, the doorbell rang.

"I'll get it," she said, jumping up as fast as

she could. She heard familiar giggling on the other side of the door. Oh, well, it sounded as if they'd forgotten all about yesterday. Stevie was ready to say something funny to the three girls as soon as she opened the door. But she didn't see them! She still heard their laughter coming from behind the hedge, but standing where Stevie expected them to be was the strangest snowman she'd ever seen. It was only half a snowman, split down the middle from top to bottom.

"Meet Mrs. Snow's Better Half, get it? Better half. Half of a snowman." Molly was laughing as she peeked around the bushes.

"Very funny," Stevie said, trying not to laugh. "And how about if I just give it half a laugh?"

"Surprise!" said Meg and Laura together, coming out from behind the hedges and brushing the snow off each other as they came.

"It's our latest creation," Laura said.

"Snow Builders at your service! This is our half-price special. For half the price, you get half the ice!" Meg was practically doubled over with laughter. And she wasn't usually the one to make the jokes.

Even Stevie felt cheered by Meg's joke. She hurried to put on her jacket and tried not to bump Mrs. Snow's Better Half with her backpack as she stepped around him. "This guy is really awesome," she said when she was standing next to the snowman. "I think we could make zillions with this kind of snow sculpture. We can make up fliers to advertise our business. We could have the ads say what Meg said, 'Half the ice for half the price.' " Stevie was getting excited about the idea of really getting the club's business going. For the moment, she forgot about the wedding, and she poured out more money-making ideas. "We could even go to the Town Hall and see if they'd want us to build a whole snow sculpture for the town!" she said enthusiastically. "We'll be rich and famous!"

"Yeah, that would be great," said Molly.

"Really," agreed Meg.

"Sure," said Laura.

"We can start after school today," said Stevie, starting to feel that things were going to be all right after all.

"Well, not today," Meg said. "We're having a meeting."

"So, after the meeting," Stevie said.

"I don't think there will be time because we have a lot of other things to talk about," Meg told her.

"What? Dresses again?" Stevie said, kicking at the snow.

"Oh, that reminds me," Meg continued. "We decided on red velvet."

"Yeah, I know," Stevie answered, deliberately stepping into the deepest snowbank. She sank up to her knees, and wished it were deeper. "Molly's mother called my mother last night and told her."

"I know," said Molly. "Julie called my mother to make sure it was all right for us to be in her wedding. So then my mom said she would call the other mothers."

"Mine said yes," Laura said, pushing her long hair back with her mittened hand.

"So did all of them," said Meg, talking about the mothers like they were in their own club. "I think they're going to get together to talk about our dresses, too."

"Well, whoopty-do," Stevie said sarcastically.

"Oh, come on, Stevie," said Molly. "Wearing a dress isn't the worst thing in the universe. And besides, you have to be happy for Julie, don't you?"

"I am," Stevie lied. Well, I *should* be, she thought to herself.

"We'll meet at lunch to make plans for the meeting," Meg announced.

"There goes my appetite," mumbled Stevie.

Molly put an arm around Stevie and tried to pull her out of the snowbank. "We're all in this thing together," she laughed, hoping to lift her friend's spirits as well as her body.

Stevie sank deeper into the snow. Molly couldn't budge her.

"Come on, you guys," Meg pleaded. "We'd better get going or we'll be late."

Stevie still would not move.

"Come on, Stevie!" Molly said as she turned to join Meg and Laura.

Stevie watched her three friends starting to leave without her. She didn't try to get out of the snowbank. Her legs felt stuck, but she didn't care. "You go ahead without me," Stevie said. "I forgot something. I'll catch up."

Meg and Laura were already walking arm in arm, and Stevie could see they were back on the subject of Julie's wedding. Molly looked back at Stevie and said, "You're sure you don't want me to wait?" She seemed torn between wanting to stay with Stevie and wanting to join Meg's and Laura's wedding conversation.

"That's all right," Stevie called after Molly. "I'll see you at school."

Molly ran through the snowy sidewalk to catch up with the other girls. Stevie waited until they were all the way at the corner before she pulled her legs out of the snow. She started to go back in the house, but stopped in front of Mrs. Snow's Better Half on her steps. Looking at him for only a few seconds, Stevie dropped her backpack at the figure's feet and ran across the yard to Molly's house. She followed her own footprints to the backyard and over the hammock stand. Her finger felt around in the icy metal tubing. At first she felt nothing. Then her finger touched a wet piece of paper. She pulled out the note she had left for Molly and saw that the ink had run down the page. The message was lost.

"That's what I thought," Stevie said out loud to herself. "She's so interested in the wedding that she didn't even remember to look in her secret note hiding place." She crumpled up the soggy note and put it in her pocket.

Stevie hurried back through the snow to her house and picked up her backpack. Now she was going to be late for school, but she didn't really care. The snowman had half a smile on his half face. Stevie smooshed it with her gloved hand.

"Wipe that smile off your face, mister," she snapped at the figure. Then, without really thinking, Stevie knocked the rest of the snowman down with her backpack.

"Take *that*, Eric T. Bowen!" she said. She swung the backpack again. "And *that*, Mr. Robert 'Bob' Reston!"

The Better Half was gone, and for some reason Stevie felt a lot better.

DINNER FOR TOO MANY

Nothing was as it should be. The snow, which was supposed to have been a gold mine for the Friends 4-Ever Club, had practically all melted. The club meetings, which were supposed to be about planning for a Valentine's Day party, were now about planning for a Valentine's Day wedding. Julie, who was supposed to be coaching Stevie in hockey, was too busy making wedding arrangements. And Bob, who was supposed to take just Stevie's mother out on dates, had invited the whole family out for dinner.

"It'd better be Chinese," said Stevie when her mother, with a big smile on her face, announced the invitation.

Mrs. Ames laughed. "Oh, Stevie," she said, "there are other restaurants to eat at besides Chinese."

The night of the big dinner, Bob arrived with a flower corsage for Mrs. Ames, and one for Stevie, too. Everyone was dressed in what Stevie called church clothes, because they were not going to an informal Chinese restaurant.

"I've made reservations at the Cafe Roval," Bob told them.

"That's so fancy!" Stevie gulped as she remembered driving by the place once and seeing a uniformed doorman offering a hand to women in fur coats as they arrived in their fancy cars. "I don't think they take kids."

Bob laughed. "You look charming this evening, Stevie. I don't think I've ever seen you in a dress before."

Stevie wanted to suggest that he take a picture so the memory would last, but she didn't want to risk being on the receiving end of one of her mother's warning glances. "Dresses aren't my thing," was all Stevie said.

"Well, I hope corsages are *your thing*," Bob said with a chuckle as he handed Stevie a box. Then he handed another box to Stevie's mother. "And here's one for you, too, Judy. I hope you like roses."

"Oh, I love roses, Bob," said Mrs. Ames as she opened the box and took out a beautiful corsage of white baby roses.

Stevie liked roses, too. But when she opened her box she found two pink carnations on a shiny silver elastic wristband. She watched Bob help her mother pin the rose corsage onto her coat, then looked in the box for her own pin.

"No, Stevie," said Bob when he saw Stevie searching without any luck. "It's a wrist corsage. You put the elastic around your wrist like a bracelet." He lifted Stevie's wrist and slipped the elastic around her hand. It itched immediately. Right away she felt a rash starting on her wrist where the elastic rubbed. When she saw the red marks she thought, Well, at least the rash matches my dress even if the flowers don't! Stevie was right. The coral-pink didn't really go well at all with her red-and-blue striped dress, but the rubbed spot on her arm matched almost exactly.

"And I even have a little something for you boys," Bob said handing each boy a white carnation. "A boutonniere for each of you."

"A boot in the ear?" Stevie repeated, just to be a wiseguy.

"Thanks, Bob," said Dave as he put the flower through his buttonhole.

Mike jumped up on the stair landing and leaned over holding out his flower. In a high voice more like a girl's than his own he said, "Time to throw the bouquet. OK, who's going to be the next lovely bride?"

Everyone had to laugh, even Stevie, but when Mike really did toss the flower into their midst, Stevie made sure she stepped in front of her mother's hand. She caught it easily. "Uh-oh, Stevie," said Dave. "Looks like you're heading for a wedding!"

"Say that again," threatened Stevie, "and you'll be cruisin' for a bruisin'!"

Bob stopped the almost-argument. "Hey, how about heading for the restaurant?"

"And here's your boot-in-the-ear," said Stevie, handing over the flower to Mike. He put it in his lapel buttonhole and then took a formal bow. Dave applauded.

"No applause," said Mike. "Just throw money, please."

The jokes flew back and forth from one Ames to another. Even Mrs. Ames got a few laughs out on the way to the restaurant in Bob's car. Bob shook his head and smiled as he drove. "I don't know," he said slowly. "You Ameses are too fast for me, I'm afraid. I feel like I'm right smack in the middle of a Marx Brothers movie."

"More like *Three Stooges*," laughed Mrs. Ames.

"Oh, Mom," said Dave, Mike, and Stevie all together.

When at last they pulled up to the restaurant and the same uniformed doorman Stevie had seen from a distance offered her his hand, Stevie got all flustered. "I can get out OK," she said. She climbed over the seatbelt strap and tripped on the way out. Luckily, the doorman caught her.

"Take it easy there, miss," said the man, tipping his hat to her.

Stevie was grateful for the darkness that hid her embarrassed face. She wasn't sure what was more embarrassing, tripping or wearing a rash-giving wrist corsage. She hardly looked up at all as the hostess showed them all to a round table in the middle of the dining room. On it was a sign that read RESERVED FOR THE RESTON PARTY, which seemed strange to Stevie since most of "the party" were Ameses.

White tablecloths, enough silverware at each place to last for a week's worth of suppers, plates on plates, two rows of glasses, a white linen napkin folded in the shape of a swan, and butter cut in the shape of little swans, all made Stevie and her brothers open their eyes wide.

Stevie elbowed her brother Mike and whispered loudly. "Something tells me we're not in Kansas anymore." She rolled her eyes left then right to show that all the fancy surroundings did not impress her one bit.

"It's lovely, isn't it?" Mrs. Ames said, mistaking Stevie's eye-rolling for admiration.

"Whoa! Look at this!" Mike exclaimed a little too loudly for the hushed surroundings of Cafe Roval. "It must be a fork for leprechauns! It's so tiny!"

"That's your seafood fork," Dave informed him. He couldn't remember where he'd picked up that bit of information, but Bob was impressed.

"Very good, Dave," he said. "So, you're a man of the world, are you?"

Stevie rolled her eyes upward this time and slumped down lower in her chair. That's when she noticed that all the napkin swans on the table were gone except hers. Before she had a chance to unfold it and put in her lap, as everyone else had done, the waiter came and unfolded it for her. He handed the napkin to her, and she quickly put it in her lap. Thank goodness no one I know is here, she thought. Then she thought about Molly, Meg, and Laura. She missed them. If they had been at the table it would have been completely different. They would have all made jokes about too many glasses, and napkins and butter shaped like swans. Stevie just knew that her friends would look around at the crystal chandeliers and know what Stevie was thinking: *Tarzan would have a great time swinging from one chandelier to the next!* Like her, they wouldn't think this place was so great. Stevie was sure of that!

The waiter put something down in front of Stevie that she was sure she didn't order and didn't want. "Your hearts-of-palm salad, *mada-moiselle*," said the waiter.

Oh, brother, thought Stevie, even the salad has hearts! What next?

"So, Stevie," Bob interrupted her thoughts, "your mother has been telling me you're quite a soccer star."

"Well, I . . . ah . . ." Stevie started to answer.

"And Dave, I gather you're not too bad at the game yourself, right?" Bob didn't really give Stevie a chance to answer. Now he didn't give Dave a chance either. "But, Mike, you're the basketball player in the family, is that right? That was always my sport, too. Used to love trying for those three-pointers from center court."

"Oh, yeah," Mike began, "I . . . ah . . ."

"Oh, I remember some pretty fast-moving games there. What position do you play, Mike?

59

I played guard. It was lots of fun. Lots of fun indeed." Bob seemed too lost in his own memories and in his hearts-of-palm salad to listen to Stevie or Dave or Mike.

"I played basketball, too," Mrs. Ames said.

"You did?" said Bob. "Well, how about that." He seemed *very* interested in hearing all about her basketball-playing days.

Stevie sat uncomfortably in the chair, which felt too big for her. The velvet-cushioned seat hit the back of her knees in the wrong spot, causing her to squirm in her seat. As she looked around at the other people sitting stiffly at their tables, smiling smiles that seemed fake to Stevie, she wondered why anyone would choose a place like this over Burger-in-a-Hurry or Quick Chicken on Main Street. At least in those places they gave out straws with the drinks!

Dinner arrived "one thing at a time," as Stevie later described it to Molly. Dave didn't seem to mind at all that the roast beef was wrapped in some kind of flaky pastry crust and there was no ketchup bottle on the table. And Mike didn't even notice that the Vegetable Medley had lima beans in it! Her brothers were too busy talking to each other, while Mrs. Ames and Bob toasted each other and talked happily about his work at the school and her work at the real estate office.

Stevie had no one to talk to and nothing to do except pick bits of parsley off the tiny round potatoes. It was the same feeling she'd had since the snow day when Julie first said she was getting married. Left out.

The waiter brought the dessert menu. As everyone read the long list of delicious-sounding desserts, they oohed and aahhed over each item. The only thing that looked good to Stevie was the Richest Chocolate Choice Cake. Maybe chocolate cake will make me feel better, she thought to herself.

When the dessert came, three surprises came with it. The first surprise was in the first bite. "Yeech!" Stevie said, dropping her fork and grabbing for her own throat.

"Stevie!" Mrs. Ames said, astonished at her daughter's chocolate-covered tongue hanging out of her mouth.

"There's poison in it or something!" Stevie gasped, swallowing the bite against her better judgment.

Bob laughed. "Oh, it's probably the rum-soaked cake. French pastries often have something extra in them."

"Something disgusting is more like it," Stevie snarled.

"Stevie!" her mother scolded. That was all she

had to say. Stevie felt the sting of her mother's angry tone.

Then came the second surprise.

"Stevie!" She heard her name again, but this time it was a friendlier voice saying it.

"Julie!" said Stevie, the first smile of the night spreading over her freckled face. "What are you doing here?"

Julie was dressed as Stevie had never seen her dressed before. The black velvet dress was certainly a change from the red shorts and white shirt that were the counselor's uniform at Camp Mohawk. "Eric and I came for dinner," Julie explained.

Then Stevie saw Eric coming up behind Julie. When they got closer to the table, Bob stood up, and Julie and Eric introduced themselves to him. "And of course we know you, Mrs. Ames. And you, too, guys," Julie said to Stevie's brothers. "You all look so nice tonight. What a beautiful corsage, Mrs. Ames."

"Stevie got one, too," Mike pointed out.

Reluctantly, Stevie held up her wrist with the wrong color of flowers on it. All she could see was the rash. All Julie could see were the carnations. "Oh, it's so sweet," Julie said, examining the carnations. "And that cake looks pretty sweet, too," she added when she looked over and saw Stevie's dessert. "Maybe we should order one of those cakes for the rehearsal dinner," she said, turning her attention to the tall, blond young man next to her. She smiled at him in a way that was as sickening to Stevie as the chocolate cake.

"Aren't they sweet together?" Stevie heard her mother whisper to Bob.

It was *all* too sweet for Stevie. Maybe a joke would help. "Don't order one of these cakes for your dinner," Stevie advised. "It's so heavy you'd never get it out of this place!"

Everyone laughed. Then Julie gave Stevie the third surprise of her night. "Well, we wouldn't have to get the cake out of 'this place.' This place is where we're having the rehearsal dinner!"

"Here?" gasped Stevie. "Why would you want to have it — "

"In the loveliest restaurant in the area," finished Mrs. Ames before Stevie could say something else.

"Yes," said Julie with a dreamy look in her eyes. She looked around at the velvet chairs, white linens, and fine china, and she sighed happily. "It really is perfect, isn't it?"

"It sure is, Julie," Bob agreed. "The perfect place for every special occasion. Like *this* special occasion," he added, looking right at Stevie's mother when he said it. Then he reached into his pocket for something.

A ring! screamed a voice inside Stevie's head. *He's going to pull out a ring and ask my mom to marry him right here in this perfect place for every special occasion!* Stevie could hardly breathe as she watched Bob's hand move in what seemed to be very slow motion. Slowly, slowly his hand came out of his pocket, and then she saw it. "A handkerchief!" she blurted out. Then she started laughing as Bob tried to discreetly turn his head and softly blow his nose into the handkerchief. Dave, Mike, her mother, Julie, and Eric all turned their eyes to Stevie to see why she was laughing. She didn't want to say that she was laughing because the ring she expected turned out to be just a handkerchief, so instead she changed the subject back to the rehearsal dinner.

"What is a rehearsal dinner, anyway?" asked Stevie.

Julie's eyes brightened as she took hold of Eric's arm and explained it to Stevie. "The rehearsal dinner is a nice party just for the people who are in the wedding and in the family. The day before the wedding we'll have a rehearsal in the church so we'll all know what we're supposed to do. Then we'll come here for dinner. Sound good?"

64

"Sounds wonderful," said Mrs. Ames.

Sounds terrible, thought Stevie. The whole idea of having to watch Julie get married in a rehearsal and then having to watch it all over again seemed bad enough. But to have to come back to celebrate in a place that didn't even have a bottle of ketchup on the table seemed worse.

Stevie wished everything would go back to the way it had been before Cupid started shooting his arrows into people close to Stevie.

Julie and Eric stayed another minute or two while Mrs. Ames and Bob listened to more of their wedding plans. Mike and Dave sat politely listening, too, but Stevie didn't want to hear any more. She wiggled in her seat, played with her napkin, and wrecked the cake with the last fork left in the place setting. Before Julie and Eric went to their table for two, Julie bent down next to Stevie and put an arm around her slumped shoulders. "Hey, Stevie," she said softly, "I'll see you tomorrow at the club meeting, OK? Meg called me and said you all want to talk about the dresses before your big shopping trip."

"What big shopping trip?" Stevie wanted to know.

"The one you're all planning together," Julie reminded her. "I'll see you tomorrow."

Good-byes were said, and Stevie watched Julie

and Eric walk through the rows of elegantly set tables to their own romantic table in a corner. While her mother and Bob had coffee, and Dave and Mike finished their desserts, Stevie sat solemnly watching the table in the corner. All her mother talked about was what a nice couple Julie and Eric were. All Bob talked about was what a nice family Stevie's mother had, and he hoped they could share a lot of evenings like this one. All Stevie thought about was *getting out of this place, out of this dress, and out of this itchy corsage.* Finally Stevie's mother noticed how restless Stevie was to go home.

"All right, Stevie Lou," said Mrs. Ames. "You can turn back into a pumpkin in a few more minutes. Everyone is finished now."

Stevie looked over again at the table in the corner. Julie and Eric had their heads together looking over the menu and choosing together what to have for dinner. She was hoping Julie would look up and give her a wave or a smile, but Eric held all her attention. Next she saw Eric lean toward Julie and kiss her! That was more than Stevie could stand. She roughly pulled her coat on over the wrist corsage, crushing the flowers completely. Before Mike, Dave, Bob, and her mother had a chance to get their own coats on, Stevie was already on her way to the door. As she walked by the table in the corner, Julie said, "See you tomorrow, Stevie," but Stevie just kept walking. "Stevie?" Julie called after her, but Stevie did not look back.

All the way home in the car, Stevie sat quietly huddled in the backseat with her face tucked into the neck of her coat so her own breath would keep her warm. Even though everyone else in the car was talking, Stevie could only hear one voice, Julie's. "See you tomorrow, Stevie," it said in her mind. "See you tomorrow, Stevie." And Stevie had not even answered. Now she felt sick to her stomach. How could she do that to Julie? Even if she did feel jealous and mad, how could she not even say good-bye? She was sure Julie's feelings must be hurt, or worse, maybe Julie was angry at Stevie.

When at last the car pulled up in front of the Ameses' house and Bob opened the door for Stevie, she felt very tired. But once she was in her pajamas and in bed, sleep would not come. It wasn't Julie's voice saying, "See you tomorrow, Stevie," that kept her awake. What kept her awake was her own silence after Julie had said that.

There was only one thing to do now and Stevie knew exactly what that was. In the bright light of the moon that shone in through her window,

Stevie wrote four notes; one to Molly, one to Meg, one to Laura, and one to Julie. First thing the next morning Stevie knew what she would do. She would put each friend's note in her secret note hiding place: Molly's in the hammock tubing, Laura's in the chimney of the birdhouse in her front yard, Meg's in the fence post by her front door — and Julie's note in Mrs. Hansen's mailbox.

All the notes said the same thing:

I've made up my mind and don't try to change it.
I'm not, I repeat NOT, going to be in the wedding.
Weddings just aren't my thing.
  Yours 'til the book jacket buttons,

  STEVIE

OUTSIDE LOOKING IN

The following morning was so beautiful that everyone should have been feeling happy and hopeful. The sky was a brilliant blue, the air was crisp and cold, and the bare branches of the trees all around Crispin Landing stood out like pen-and-ink artwork against blue canvas.

Stevie didn't notice any of the beauty. She was intent on delivering her notes to their secret hiding places before anyone got up. It had always been their habit, ever since Molly came back after a year away in Kansas, to share their thoughts through notes. Just for fun they left notes for each other, and they all checked the note places everyday — or at least they were supposed to.

Stevie ran first to Molly's, then to Laura's, then to Meg's, and finally to Mrs. Hansen's house. By the time she finished, Crispin Landing was just starting to come to life. The smell of bacon cooking drifted out of some houses, smoke curled from several chimneys, early-rising children were already outside playing.

"At least *some* people will enjoy the day," Stevie said as she jogged around the corner and up her own street. The secret note habit made her stop at the best climbing tree in Crispin Landing to check in the hollowed-out branch that was her note place. She reached a hand in and pulled out a note with the familiar rainbow design across the top.

Dear Stevie,
We all took turns trying to call you last night, but there was no answer. So I ran out to put this note in your tree. It's important for you to know that we are planning the biggest, best shopping trip ever. We're all going to meet at Meg's house. Then Julie will

walk with us to Annette's Bridal Salon in town. After we pick out our dresses, we'll all have lunch at the Yellow Brick Road. I hope you get this note, but I'll call you in the morning just to be sure. It's going to be so, so, so much fun! See you at Meg's at 9:30 sharp.

Friends 4 Keeps,

Molly

Uh-oh, thought Stevie. Now what? She opened the front door to her house as quietly as possible. Her mother was in the kitchen, singing as usual, and didn't hear Stevie come in. Stevie crept up the stairs more quietly than she'd ever crept before. She took off her jacket and her clothes, put her pajamas back on, and got back in bed. It wasn't a minute too soon. The phone rang. Mrs. Ames picked it up, and Stevie could hear her saying, "Oh hi, Molly. Just a minute, all right? I'm not even sure she's up yet." Then she heard her mother put the phone down on the kitchen counter while she came softly up the stairs and peeked in at Stevie who seemed to be asleep. She went back downstairs and reported her findings to Molly. "We had a late night last night, Molly, and I guess Stevie is sleeping in this morning. May I take a message?" Pause. "Uh-huh . . . yes . . . Okay . . . yes . . . Sure, I'll be glad to tell her. Meet you and the other girls at Annette's Bridal Salon at ten sharp unless she gets up in time to meet you at Meg's at nine-thirty. OK, honey, I've got it and I'll tell her, but I can't imagine her sleeping much longer. Stevie's never been one to stay in bed once the sun is up."

Stevie heard her mother say good-bye and hang up, then the singing started again. Of course Stevie didn't feel a bit tired, but the last thing she wanted to do this morning was go shopping for a dress to wear in a wedding she wasn't even going to be in. She wondered what all her friends would say when they got their notes. She wondered if Julie was still mad at her for not saying good-bye when she left the res-taurant. She wondered if things would ever be back to the way they were. And as the clock ticked closer and closer to 10:00 A.M., Stevie even began to wonder what would be going on at Annette's Bridal Salon. Curiosity got the best of her, and for the second time that morning she got out of bed, put her clothes on, and went downstairs.

"Stevie!" sang her mother. "Well, you sure are a slugabed this morning. Too much fancy food and fancy fun last night, huh? Well, I'm glad you could sleep. Here," she said handing Stevie a crushed-looking carnation corsage. "I put this in the refrigerator to keep it fresh for you. I thought you might want to show it to the girls."

"First I would show them *this*," Stevie said, holding up a wrist ringed in red rash.

"Oh, dear," said Mrs. Ames. "I guess the band rubbed you the wrong way."

"I guess everything rubbed her the wrong way last night," Mike added as he came clomping into the kitchen carrying his skates over his shoulder and a hockey stick in his hand. "Especially Bob."

"Oh, Bob's all right," defended Mrs. Ames. "He means well, and it was awfully nice of him to treat us all to such a nice evening out."

"I don't know why he bothered to take us," Stevie complained. "He only talked to you the whole night."

"Well, never mind that now, Stevie," her mother said. "Molly called this morning and wants you to meet her and the rest of the girls at Annette's Bridal Salon. Mike's going to play ice hockey on the mill pond, so you two could walk over there together."

"I'm not showing my face in some bride dress store," Mike exclaimed.

"You don't have to go in, Mike," Mrs. Ames explained patiently with a laugh.

"That'll be perfect," said Stevie. She had no plans to go inside the store, either, but she did want to see what her friends were doing. She wanted to see just how much they missed her.

When Stevie and Mike arrived at the store, Mike was in a hurry to get to the mill pond and get away from anything to do with brides' dresses. " 'Bye, Stevarino," he said as he left her there. "Don't buy anything I wouldn't buy."

"Don't worry," Stevie called after him. "I won't." Then she turned to the store window and saw three brides all dressed in white with paper hearts hanging down from the ceiling, giving the impression that it was raining hearts. Stevie pressed her face up against the glass and shaded her eyes so she could see in. At first all she saw were mannequins wearing different styles of wedding dresses. There were also several smaller mannequins wearing different-colored short dresses. These, Stevie figured out, must be junior bridesmaids and flower girls. As she breathed on the glass of the window and fogged it up with her own breath, she was suddenly surprised to see one of the mannequins moving! It wasn't a mannequin after all — it was Laura!

Stevie quickly stepped away from the window so no one inside the store could see her. Slowly and carefully she peeked in the window again. Now she saw two other moving mannequins, Molly and Meg. Each girl had on a different style of red dress and each style made Stevie gasp in more horror than the last. All the dresses looked too big. Right before her very eyes were her very best friends in the whole world dressed in dresses that made them look like little Miss Americas. Meg's yellow curls were piled high on her head in a way that Stevie thought made her look like a Barbie Doll's little sister, whose hair had gotten caught in an electric ceiling fan. Laura twirled around in a dress with a skirt so wide Stevie thought it would knock over lamps and furniture. And Molly gave Stevie the biggest shock of all when she came out wearing a dress that had layers and layers of red taffeta. She looked like an icing flower on an ice-cream cake, which in Stevie's opinion was OK for a cake, but definitely not OK for Molly. Not one of the dresses looked right.

Stevie kept watching, and through the door

she could hear the excited cries of delight coming from her friends as they admired each other and themselves.

"Oh, Meg," Molly said excitedly, "you look beautiful!"

"So do you," Meg returned the compliment.

"So do you, Laura," Molly gushed to her friend.

"So do you all," said Julie as she stepped out from behind a curtain, wearing the most beautiful wedding gown any of the girls had ever seen. Julie looked perfect. Even Stevie had to admit it.

Julie seemed to float across the room like Cinderella at the ball. The girls gathered around her like the mice in the attic as Meg held out her train, Laura held onto a part of the long skirt, and Molly reached to straighten the simple satin headpiece from which a long veil floated down. Not a thing seemed to be missing, but of course, something was. Stevie was missing. But no one was missing Stevie. That was very clear to her as she dared to press her face up to the glass again. Her friends were doing turns in front of the triple mirrors as they all giggled and felt the material of each others' dresses. They didn't see Stevie, and they also didn't seem able to see themselves as Stevie saw them! To her eyes, only

Julie really looked beautiful. Her other friends only looked like little girls playing dress-up. Surely they weren't really planning to buy any of these dresses, Stevie hoped.

"Oh, well," she muttered out loud, "what do I care what dresses they buy? I'm not going to be in the wedding anyway." A loud gale of laughter brought her thoughts back to the scene inside the store. Stevie had to cover her mouth to hold in her own laughter when she saw what was going on.

"Oh, Meg!" laughed Laura. "What happened?"

Stevie saw exactly what had happened. Meg's curls, which had been piled so high on her head, had slipped down to one side so they were sticking out and made her look very funny. As Meg's hair fell, so did the shoulders of her dress, which was really much too big for her. Standing before the mirrors, Meg caught three identical images of herself looking as though she were falling apart. Now she could see that the dress really wasn't right for her. Disappointment clouded Meg's face.

To make Meg feel better, the other girls decided against their dresses, too. "Too puffy," said Molly about her layer-cake look.

"Too wide," Laura criticized her own dress.

"Too bad," said Julie about all of the dresses. "Maybe stores just won't carry dresses that are really right for you all. And can you imagine what Stevie would say about any of these dresses?"

The girls in their wrong dresses all laughed at the thought. "Stevie!" said Molly, suddenly noticing her friend's absence. "She didn't come. I hope she got the message."

"Well, in a way it's just as well if she doesn't come," Meg said, looking at her disheveled image in the mirrors. "Ugh!" she groaned. "One of me is bad enough, but three of me! I've got to get out of this thing!"

Annette, the dark-haired and jolly owner of the store, came out from behind the curtain then and led Meg back to the dressing rooms. Stevie wondered what Meg meant when she said it was just as well if Stevie didn't come? Maybe Julie had told them about what Stevie had done at the restaurant. Maybe now they were *all* mad at her! And maybe when they got her notes saying she wasn't going to be in Julie's wedding, they would think that was just as well, too.

"And maybe it *is* just as well," she said out loud. She turned to leave but then heard Meg's voice again.

"What will we do now, Julie?" Meg was calling

out from behind the curtained dressing room.

"It's too early to eat, I think," Julie said, removing the veiled headpiece from her head.

"No, I mean about dresses. Does this mean we can't be in the wedding?" Meg was obviously pulling the dress over her head when she said this. Stevie could hear how muffled her voice sounded. Meg also sounded very worried.

"Don't worry," Julie said.

Laura and Molly dragged themselves in their oversized dresses behind the curtain to talk with Meg. Julie followed, leaving the front room of the store empty of moving models. All that was left there were the stiff, smiling brides standing forever frozen in their plaster poses. For some reason Stevie took a similiar pose outside the store door. She stuck one hand out gracefully and held the other hand at her waist. She tipped her head and smiled a fake smile. After all, she thought, I might as well just be a mannequin since no one pays any attention to them, either. Her friends' laughter brought her back to life. Quickly she broke the pose and went to hide behind the bushes on the side of Annette's Bridal Salon. She heard Annette's French accent calling after the girls as they left her shop, "*Au revoir*, good-bye. I am so sorry we could not find just zee right thing. You come back again, though, *oui*?"

"Yes, *oui*," said Julie. "*Merci, madame*, thank you so much."

Stevie could see perfectly from her spot in the bushes. Her friends all looked normal again in their regular clothes, the way Stevie liked them to look. She would have rather been standing with them than squatting alone in the bushes.

Julie looked at her watch. "Well, maybe it's not too early after all. By the time we all got out of those dresses, it really is just about lunchtime. Shall we continue on to the Yellow Brick Road then?"

"I know I can eat," Molly said, adjusting her cowboy boots, which she'd taken to wearing ever since horses became her first love while she lived in Kansas.

"Same," said Meg, fluffing up her curls and hoping they looked better down than sticking out of the side of her head.

Laura didn't say anything. She was obviously lost in some daydream.

"Laura?" Julie said. "Hungry?"

"Oh! Yes, sure. I was just thinking about how beautiful you'll look on your wedding day. I can't wait to be walking behind you, watching your long train sweeping the church aisle as we go. It will be so romantic."

"Too bad *we'll* be naked!" Meg said.

"Meg!" Molly gasped. "We won't be naked!"

"We will be if we don't have any dresses," explained Meg.

The others laughed. "You'll have dresses." Julie smiled. "Don't worry about that. In fact, I have an idea I think will work out perfectly. Maybe store-bought isn't the best answer in this case."

"You mean, we'll make them?" Molly said. "I can't even sew a button on without sticking my finger with the needle. Of course if the material is red, a little blood from my finger won't matter much." She giggled at her own joke.

The girls were walking away from where Stevie was hidden, and about all she could hear now was a lot of laughter. It sounded as if they were having a lot of fun without her. She peeked out from behind the bushes and saw the group turning the corner and heading in the direction of all the girls' favorite eating place, the Yellow Brick Road.

Maybe she could still join them for lunch, Stevie decided. She hurried after them, running past the Cozy Donut Shop, Mr. Dimitri's Flower Shop, and Park's Laundry. She had almost caught up to them when she heard Julie say, "Oh, I'm sure she'll want to do it. Just because she wasn't with us at the store doesn't mean she isn't eager to be involved in every part of the wedding."

"She really is terrific," Molly said.

"The best in the world," Meg added.

Suddenly Stevie felt a lot better. Maybe they weren't mad at her after all. But what was it they were so sure she would want to do? And if they thought she was so eager to be involved in every part of the wedding, should she hurry back to get the notes before they found them? Then Molly said something else.

"Yes, Mrs. Hansen is absolutely the most terrific, best-in-the-world seamstress I've ever known. She'll be able to make dresses for us that will be exactly what we want."

Stevie's happiness disappeared as she realized that the girls hadn't been talking about her at all. All along it had been Mrs. Hansen. She stayed hidden behind the yellow bricks that stuck out on the side of the restaurant, and slid down into a sitting position with her back to the wall. This time she didn't bother to watch her friends walking into the restaurant. Instead, she gave them time to get far enough ahead so she wouldn't have to hear any more laughter, or any more talk about a wedding that she would have nothing to do with at all.

WHAT WEDDING?

Dear Stevie,
We've always been best best friends
And so I hope you'll say
The thoughts you had when you wrote your
  note
Are not still true today.
You have to change your mind now
And say it isn't true

Julie's wedding won't be complete
If we don't have you.
            Friends 'til snowballs bounce,

Molly

Dear Stevie,
Ever since I found your note in the chimney
of my birdhouse I have been feeling so sad. I
don't understand, well, none of us under-
stands why you would want to be left out of
the most important day of Julie's life, and
the most exciting event of our lives (so far!).
Please change your mind. Friends 4-Ever
stick together, remember? We need you!!!!
!!!!!!!!!!!!!!!!!!!!!

            Your friend forever,

Laura

Stephanie "Stevie" Ames,

What do you mean you aren't going to be in the wedding? Of course you are! Everything has already been planned for four junior bridesmaids. Nothing will look right with only three. And nothing will feel right, either.

If you're positive that your mind is made up, unmake *it. We won't take no for an answer, and we won't take maybe, either. We* will *take* you, *though. See you at the next meeting, which is tomorrow.* Be there! *No ifs, ands, or buts about it,*

Meg

The notes had been spread out, then folded up again, then spread out on Stevie's bed again every day for two weeks. Each time she read them, she changed her mind about how she felt, only to change it back again.

Julie hadn't written a note. Instead she had

called and tried to find out why Stevie didn't want to share her big day with her. "Are you mad at me, Stevie?" she asked. "You didn't even say good-bye when you left the restaurant. Then I found this note from you."

"Am *I* mad at you?" said Stevie. "Oh, no, Julie, I could never be mad at you." Then she paused as the picture of Eric kissing Julie at the table came back to her. "I just didn't want to bother you and Eric, that's all. That's why I didn't say good-bye."

"And are you afraid you'll 'bother' Eric and me if you're in the wedding?" Julie said kiddingly.

Stevie didn't answer right away. Then she simply said, "I don't really like dresses that much."

"Oh, I see," Julie said patiently, waiting for a better excuse.

"And I'm not really good at walking slowly, you know, like the way we would have to walk." Stevie waited for Julie's response.

"Yes, I see," said Julie.

"And besides, you know I'll just ruin the way the whole wedding looks with my straggly hair and all." Stevie hoped Julie would just accept this last excuse.

"Stevie," Julie said kindly, "you know my

wedding day is going to be a very important day for me, and it is important to me to have you there. But I understand how you feel, and I'm sure Molly, Laura, and Meg will understand, too."

Understand and probably be glad, too, thought Stevie, remembering how Meg had said it was just as well Stevie wasn't with them at the dress shop.

"But do me a favor," Julie continued. "Don't make up your mind for absolute certain yet, OK? Think about it. I can't have a wedding without my little sister, can I?"

And what will I have without my big sister? Stevie thought sadly. A wedding day was supposed to be a happy day. But for Stevie, Julie's wedding day was sure to be the saddest day of her life. "Down the aisle and out of our lives completely," she remembered her own words. Even now that some time had passed since she first heard the news, Stevie still had not gotten used to the idea of Julie McCarthy being Julie Bowen.

Since the phone call from Julie and the notes from Molly, Laura, and Meg, Stevie had found lots of reasons to stay away from her friends. Or maybe they were staying away from her. Stevie wasn't really sure. At first the girls took turns trying to talk Stevie into coming to meetings so she would be in on the plans for what gift the Friends 4-Ever would give to Julie and Eric. Stevie suddenly had a new interest in watching Mike and his friends play ice hockey on the mill pond. Once she even chose to go to a museum with her mother and Bob!

"Sorry," said Stevie when Molly called for one meeting. "Can't. I have plans."

Laura called another day. "Hi, Stevie," she said, friendly and sweet as ever. "We're all meeting at Mrs. Hansen's house to work on dresses. She's making them. Don't you even want to come and look?"

"Sorry," Stevie said again this time. "Can't. I already have plans."

Finally Meg called. "Stevie Ames, this is an official announcement. You are in the club and part of the responsibility of being a club member is to come to club meetings. We have had exactly four formal meetings and three informal ones and you have not attended any of them. Today we're having a meeting . . ."

Stevie was just about to say, "Can't," but Meg continued.

". . . and Julie's coming."

"Julie?" Stevie said.

"That's right, Julie. She's coming to see how

the dresses look on us and to talk to us about the rehearsal and rehearsal dinner. Even though you don't want to be in the wedding, you still want to be in the club, I hope!"

"Well, of course I do," Stevie stammered, surprised that Meg might think such a thing. "I never meant I didn't want to be in the club. I've just been busy."

"Busy being busy, I think you mean," Meg said in an impatient voice.

"Well, anyway, where is the meeting? I might as well come and see how you're all going to look." Stevie softened her tone a little, even though Meg had not.

"At Mrs. Hansen's house — " Meg began.

"Again?" Stevie interrupted.

"Again." Meg repeated. "We're all having the final fitting of our dresses and discussing what to wear to the rehearsal dinner at Cafe Roval."

Just the mention of the restaurant's name made Stevie rub her wrist. But it was her feelings that hurt. The memory of seeing her mother having such a good time with Bob and seeing Julie actually *k-i-s-s-i-n-g* Eric made Stevie feel even worse. "Oh," she said to Meg, "my favorite restaurant."

"I'm sure it will be a whole different thing if you're there with Molly, Laura, and me," Meg assured Stevie. "Julie said the rehearsal dinner is one of the nicest parts of a wedding because it's a smaller group. You know, just the ones closest to the bride and groom. Julie said the guest list for the wedding and reception is growing and growing. She said it's mostly Eric's family's friends and people she doesn't even know. And Julie said — "

"Julie said! Julie said! Julie said! All right, all right, I'll come to the meetings and hear it all for myself so you don't have to keep saying 'Julie said, Julie said,' " laughed Stevie. "As long as you promise and make the others promise not to try to change my mind about being in the wedding."

"I don't understand you, Stevie Ames. This is going to the best — "

Stevie interrupted Meg again. "Promise, or I'm not coming."

"OK," Meg gave in. "I promise."

"Cross your eyes?" Stevie asked.

First Meg rolled her eyes in exasperation, then she crossed them and said, "Cross my eyes," as a sign of her solemn promise.

When Stevie stopped by Molly's house on the way to the meeting, she was surprised to see Molly's arms full of party dresses, tights, hair ribbons, barrettes, and party shoes. "Oh, good,

Stevie," Molly said as she tried to open the door without dropping the clothes. "Here, would you hold these for a minute?" She piled them all into Stevie's arms so that Stevie's face was completely hidden behind them.

"What are we going to, a Paris fashion show or something?" Stevie shifted the pile to the other arm and blew a piece of hair out of her mouth. She saw the smoke of her own breath in the chilly February air and hugged the clothes closer for warmth.

"It's more like a Crispin Landing fashion show," Molly said. "The wedding is only three days away, and we still haven't decided what we're wearing to the rehearsal dinner."

"Oh," Stevie said sadly. Only three more days until life would be permanently changed. Stevie looked up and saw snow clouds gathering. It reminded her of the day that started out so happily when the Snow Busters were starting their big money-making jobs. She wished she could turn back the clock and start all over again. She would still want the Snow Busters to be working in Mrs. Hansen's driveway. She would still want Mrs. Hansen to come out with hot cocoa and heart-shaped cookies. And she would still want Julie to come driving up, greeting her with a big big-sister hug. But if she could change just one thing, it would be what Julie had said that day: "I'm getting married."

As Molly and Stevie walked to Mrs. Hansen's house, Molly was so full of excited chatter she forgot to take back the pile of clothes. The whole way there, Stevie carried them, trying her best to peek out from behind the puffy skirts and sleeves.

"I can't believe it's all going to be happening in only three days!" Molly was saying.

Stevie opened her mouth to say something and got a mouthful of material.

"Even if you're not going to be *in* it, Stevie, you'll be there, won't you?" Molly went on unaware that Stevie was struggling to walk, talk, and see over the dresses all at the same time.

"First we'll have the rehearsal," Molly bubbled. "Oh, gosh, I hope I don't trip or do something totally embarrassing."

As if on cue, Stevie tripped, and Molly grabbed onto her arm in time to save her. "Stevie! Watch where you're going!" Molly laughed.

"I would if I could see over all this stuff," Stevie sputtered.

"Ohmigosh!" said Molly, suddenly seeing Stevie buried beneath her clothes. "I'm sorry! I was talking so much I forgot you were holding my stuff. But it's not heavy." She reached to take the things from Stevie's arms.

"Easy for you to say," Stevie said sarcastically. "I just carried it almost all the way here!" They were walking up to Mrs. Hansen's door when it opened and Mrs. Hansen greeted them.

"Molly, honey," said the woman, "that's too much for you to carry all this way! Stevie, can't you help her a little?"

Both girls started laughing and that brought Laura and Meg to the door to see what was so funny. Seeing the audience, Stevie immediately started hanging onto Molly's clothes-filled arms making her burden heavier. And Molly groaned loudly, acting as though she was carrying a grand piano.

Mrs. Hansen let the two clowning girls in and took the load of clothing from Molly's arms. "Follow the other girls into the living room, and I'll be right with you. I have something I have to finish doing in the kitchen," she said. "I'll just put these in the library, and I'll join you in a minute."

Right away Meg, Laura, and Molly tried to fill Stevie in on all she'd missed: the selection of the material for the dresses, the selection of the crystal candlesticks for the wedding present, trying on Julie's headpiece and veil (they'd all had a turn playing bride), and of course all the practicing of how they would walk down the aisle.

Stevie tried to pretend she wasn't really interested, but at the mention of Julie's name she perked up. "I thought you said Julie was coming to this meeting. Isn't she here?"

"She had to go somewhere with Eric this morning, then she was planning to meet us here," Meg said. "She'll be here soon, I'm sure."

"I think she said they were going over the seating arrangements for the rehearsal dinner," Laura added.

"And the guest list, again," said Meg. "If it's as long as Julie says it is she'll be gone for hours!"

"There!" sang Mrs. Hansen gaily as she joined the girls in the living room. "Now we can start with the dresses. You girls can go in the library and start trying on your choices for the rehearsal dinner. Stevie, you and I can help be the judges as the girls come out and show us their dresses, all right?"

"Oh, I'm a great judge of dresses," Stevie said. "If it has a skirt instead of legs, I vote no."

All the girls laughed as they hurried past Stevie into the library where Mrs. Hansen had neatly laid out all the dresses the girls had brought over. Laura closed the door, and Stevie could hear giggling coming from inside the room. Mrs. Hansen saw the look on Stevie's face and knew what she was feeling. The kind woman put an arm around Stevie's shoulder and pulled her close. "Stevie," she said softly, "you don't need to be out here if you don't want to be, you know. Your friends would be a lot happier if you were in there with them."

Another gaggle of giggles could be heard coming from behind the library door. The girls sounded happy enough without her, thought Stevie, no matter what Mrs. Hansen said. Stevie wasn't changing her mind even though the laughter was tempting her. The door opened, and out stepped Laura wearing a pretty pink wool dress with pleats across the top. Her long brown hair was pulled back in a pink velvet ribbon.

Meg was right behind her wearing a bright blue dress with a square lace collar in front and back. Her shoes matched exactly, and her curly blonde hair had one barrette in it with blue, yellow, and white ribbons hanging down from it. She twirled around to give the judges a better look.

Molly came next wearing a red sailor dress with black trim. Because she was the only one with pierced ears, she had on a pair of small red button earrings that stood out brightly against her short dark hair. No cowboy boots this time for Molly. Just plain black patent-leather shoes.

Stevie and Mrs. Hansen looked up at the girls as they modeled their first choice dresses. Mrs. Hansen applauded and said, "Lovely! You all look lovely!"

Stevie was a little harder to please. She stroked her chin as she slowly walked around each girl, touched the material of each dress, adjusted Meg's collar, straightened Laura's ribbon, and adjusted Molly's sleeve. "Not too bad," she finally said, closing one eye and taking an artist's view.

"We have all the others to try on, too," Molly said, "so don't use up all your best comments on these."

"We have to show Julie, too, don't we?" Laura asked. "Is she here yet?"

"Not yet, dear," said Mrs. Hansen. "And it is getting late. I have a surprise for you all and was hoping Julie would be here for it, too."

"A surprise?" Molly said. "What is it?"

"Why don't you girls try on the rest of your dresses, then I want you to try on the ones I made for you. If Julie hasn't arrived by then, we'll just go ahead without her, all right?" Mrs. Hansen looked out the window just to see if Julie might be coming up the driveway. There was no sign of her yet.

The morning slipped away quickly as the girls tried on the other clothes they had brought. Stevie and Mrs. Hansen patiently watched the fashion show, giving their honest opinions about each outfit. The girls tried on their own dresses, and then they tried on each others'. At last the judges voted that the first ones they'd all tried on were really the best for the occasion.

"Now put on your bridesmaid dresses, girls, and let's show Stevie how nice you'll all look for the wedding," Mrs. Hansen said.

The girls disappeared into the library again, and came out wearing three identical dresses that even Stevie had to admit were beautiful. The red velvet dresses had simple long sleeves with pearl buttons holding the cuffs closed. Tiny pearls were sewn all along the neckline. There was nothing overly fancy or overdone about the dresses. They were perfect.

"You guys look really beautiful," Stevie said sincerely. "Mrs. Hansen, you really know how to handle a needle and thread!"

"Well, I have good little models to work on," laughed Mrs. Hansen. "Not a wiggler in the bunch! But now, I'm afraid we'll have to go on

97

with the surprise even if Julie isn't here."

Stevie felt disappointed. All morning she'd been hoping that Julie would get there.

"What is the surprise, Mrs. Hansen?" Molly asked.

"Come into the dining room and you'll see," said Mrs. Hansen, leading the way.

"Oh!" gasped Meg. "A Valentine's Day party!"

"Oh, Mrs. Hansen!" cried Molly. "You're incredible!"

"Everything looks so beautiful," Laura said, leaning across the table to get a closer look at the lovely, lacy hearts and flower decorations. The table was covered in white lace. Sprinkled down the center of the table were red candy hearts, and hanging from the ceiling were all different sized hearts. The table was filled with delicious-looking foods. There were heart-shaped tea sandwiches filled with cream cheese and strawberry jam. Next to them were carrot sticks and celery sticks cut and arranged to look like flowers. Plates filled with heart-shaped cookies and candies sat next to a shimmering heart-shaped strawberry-Jell-O-molded salad. And in the center of the table was the most beautiful valentine cake the girls had ever seen. It was heart-shaped, of course, with icing drizzled like a lacy doily around the edges. In the middle of the cake there were two figures of a bride and groom. The writing on the cake read, *Happy Valentine's Day Wedding.*

Amidst the "oohs and aahhs" none of them heard the front door open. When she saw the cake, Molly said happily, "The cake is just as beautiful as the wedding will be!"

They all turned around in surprise when they heard Julie, behind them say, "What wedding? I'm afraid there isn't going to be any wedding after all!"

The girls in their junior bridesmaids' dresses stood with their mouths open unable to speak. Mrs. Hansen put her hand up to her face in shock. And Stevie wondered if her secret wish was coming true.

STEVIE TO THE RESCUE

Julie's announcement that there wasn't going to be a wedding after all was as much of a surprise to everyone as her first announcement that there *was* going to be a wedding. At first no one said anything. No one knew what to say.

Tears rolled down Julie's freckled cheeks as she tried to explain what had happened. Through sobs she poured out her story. "Eric and I had a fight," she cried. "All I said was that the guest list was getting too long, and I was afraid I wouldn't know most of the people at my own wedding. Then he said these people were all friends of his family. Then I said what I really wanted was a small wedding. Then he said that maybe I just didn't want to have any wedding. Then I said, Well, maybe that would be a good idea!"

Mrs. Hansen put both arms around Julie and patted her back. "There, there, dear," she said soothingly. "You're both just a little nervous, that's all. All the plans have just made you tired."

"No," insisted Julie, "Eric's changed. Or maybe I've changed. I don't know. But it doesn't matter now because the wedding is off!" With that, Julie turned and ran crying up to her room.

The girls didn't know what to do. Suddenly they felt foolish standing there all dressed in clothes made for a wedding that wasn't going to happen.

"Oh, our beautiful dresses," Meg said. "All that work you did, Mrs. Hansen!"

"But poor Julie," said Laura thoughfully. "I've never seen her cry before."

"I feel so bad," Molly said sadly. "About Julie, about the dresses, about everything."

Stevie didn't say anything. All she could think about was what she'd been thinking about earlier. Hadn't she wished she could turn the clock back and change just one thing? And now didn't it appear that her wish was coming true?

The phone rang, and Mrs. Hansen went into

the kitchen to answer it. "Oh, Eric," she said sweetly. "Yes, Julie's here, but she's quite upset right now." The girls listened carefully, wishing they could hear Eric's side of the conversation as well. "I know, dear," Mrs. Hansen was saying. "I'm sure she didn't mean it, either." There was silence in the kitchen, then, "Yes. Yes. Well, shall I tell her you're on the phone? All right. Hold on, please." Mrs. Hansen put down the phone and came through the dining room past the girls. She didn't say anything, but just went to the bottom of the stairs and called up to Julie.

"Julie, dear, Eric is on the phone," Mrs. Hansen said.

Julie called back down the stairs. "Tell him I'm not here! Tell him I don't want to talk to him. Not now — not ever!"

"Oh, dear," the girls heard Mrs. Hansen say softly to herself on her way back to the phone. "Eric?" she said when she picked up the phone again. "I'm afraid Julie can't come to the phone right now. No, I'm sorry, she just isn't quite up to talking at this moment. Yes, dear. I'll tell her you'll call later. Now, don't you worry. Everything will be just fine."

When Mrs. Hansen came into the dining room, she found the girls looking nervous and worried. "This is so terrible," Meg said. "I feel like I'm caught in the middle of a soap opera on TV."

"But this is *real*," Molly said.

"Too real," Laura added.

"Why don't you girls get out of your dresses now and run along home while I talk to Julie. I'll wrap up some cookies and cake for you each to take and maybe you can have a little party, anyway." Mrs. Hansen began gathering up all the heart-shaped goodies so the girls wouldn't go home empty-handed, and the girls went into the library.

Stevie watched with mixed feelings. Up to now all the hearts had just served as reminders that her own heart was about to be broken. Suddenly things were changing. Stevie looked at the Valentine's Day wedding cake and saw the bride and groom still standing ready for their wedding ceremony to begin. But when Mrs. Hansen lifted the cake from the table to carry it into the kitchen, both plastic figures fell face-first into the icing. Stevie could see that Mrs. Hansen's hands were full, and something made her feel that she must save the bride and groom.

"Here," said Stevie, reaching across the cake and carefully lifting the figures up again. "I'll get them back on their feet again."

Meg, Molly, and Laura came out of the library

wearing their regular clothes again but not their regular smiles. Stevie saw the look of disappointment and worry on her friends' faces. The last time all of them had looked this sad, at the same time, was the day Molly had announced that she was moving to Kansas. But this time it's my fault, she thought. All because of me and my stupid wish!

As the girls sadly took their packages of Valentine's Day goodies from Mrs. Hansen and said their good-byes, Mrs. Hansen gave each of them a hug. "Things usually work out for the best," she said as she waved from the doorway. "You can leave your dresses here for now. Why don't you stop by tomorrow morning and then you can get your things?" Then she closed the door, leaving the girls to go on their way.

"This is the worst day of my life," said Meg dramatically.

"It's even worse for Julie," Laura said. "We just miss the wedding, but she misses the whole marriage!"

"I feel bad for Eric, too. It sounded like he was sorry," Molly said.

"Well, sorry won't do any good if Julie never hears it," said Meg matter-of-factly.

The rest of the way home Meg, Molly, and Laura talked about all the plans they'd made that would never happen now. Only Stevie seemed to have nothing to say. The other girls just figured that she was quiet because to her missing the wedding didn't mean much anyway. But Stevie was quiet because she was thinking. When they got to the corner of Laura's street, Laura said good-bye and went home. Molly and Stevie walked Meg to her house, then kept going to their own street.

"Stevie?" Molly asked when they were alone. "Are you all right? You've been quiet ever since Julie came home."

"I'm just thinking, that's all," said Stevie. "Thinking and planning."

"Planning what?" Molly wondered. "More money-making ideas now that the wedding is off?"

"Not exactly," said Stevie mysteriously as they reached her house. Stevie was in a hurry to get inside. She had something important to do. "I'll talk to you later, Molly, OK?" she said, hurrying up the steps to her door.

Molly gave Stevie a curious look, but left saying, "See ya later, Stevie."

When Stevie went inside she heard a man's voice coming from the kitchen. It was Bob. Him again! thought Stevie. I just wish . . . But this time Stevie stopped her wish before it was fully thought out. She wasn't taking any chances!

"Hi, Mr. Reston, I mean Bob," Stevie said when she came in. "How's school going?"

Bob and Stevie's mother both looked surprised. That was the most Stevie had ever said to Bob unless he asked her a question first. "Well, Stevie," Bob said in a friendly tone, "school is just fine, thank you. And how are things with you?" He looked right at Stevie and seemed genuinely interested in hearing her answer.

Stevie smiled and meant what she said when she answered, "Things are just fine with me, too. In fact, things are going to be absotively posolutely super." For the first time in a long time Stevie felt happy. She had a plan, and if her plan worked the way she hoped it would, things really would be super for her and for everyone. "I'll talk to you later, okay, Bob?" she said nicely. "There's something I have to do right now." Before Bob or her mother had a chance to say anything, Stevie had flipped her hair out of her face and headed for the stairs to her room. As she usually did when she was in a hurry, Stevie took the steps two and three at a time. She rushed into her room and quickly shut the door. The last thing I need right now is Mike or

Dave walking in on me when I'm in the middle of this! she thought.

For the next couple of hours Stevie stayed in her room. From his room, Mike could hear Stevie opening and closing drawers, climbing on a chair to get something out of her closet, pulling things out of her desk drawer, and making all kinds of sounds that were sure to add up to a big mess in her room. But the strangest sound of all, was the sound of Stevie Ames singing sweetly, "Here comes the the bride, all dressed in white . . ."

Finally, her mother called, "Dinner! Stevie! Mike! Dave!" and Stevie had to stop what she was doing. All the questions from her mother, who wondered what had put Stevie in such a good mood that she was even pleasant to Bob, and from Mike, who wondered why Stevie was singing a song she hated, didn't get answered.

"You're up to something, Stevarino," said Dave, reaching for the ketchup.

"Well, whatever it is, so far I like it," Mrs. Ames laughed.

"May I be excused?" Stevie asked with a mischievous look on her freckled face. "I hate to eat and run, but I gotta run!" She picked up her plate, carried it to the kitchen, and then ran back

107

up to her room. Once again she closed the door and went back to what she was doing before her mother had called her for dinner. She didn't know if her idea would work, but it was worth a try.

When she finished, she stood back and looked at her work. "Perfect!" she said out loud. Before her were two of the prettiest, fanciest, most special-looking heart-shaped valentines ever created. Both of the valentines had the same simple message written over the lacy doily background. The message read: *I love you and want to marry you*. On one of them Stevie wrote the name *Eric* and on the other she wrote *Julie*.

She had it all planned. The next morning she would hurry over to Mrs. Hansen's house to hand-deliver the valentine signed *Eric*. Then she would run over to Eric's house and hand-deliver the one signed *Julie*.

"A perfect plan for a perfect couple," Stevie sang out happily.

But before Stevie could call it a night, she had one more thing to do. On her special blue high-top sneaker stationery, she wrote three identical notes.

Dear Molly,
  The wedding is on!
      Yours 'til the wedding rings,

STEViE

Dear Meg,
The wedding is on!
    Yours 'til the wedding rings,

STEViE

Dear Laura,
The wedding is on!
        Yours 'til the wedding rings,

            STEVIE

HERE COMES THE
BRIDE . . . AND STEVIE!

"You're a genius, Stevie Ames," Meg was saying as she pushed open Stevie's bedroom door.

"An absolute incredible Einstein!" Molly added.

"A lifesaver, really," Laura said, following Molly into the room.

Stevie wasn't surprised to see her friends or to hear their praise. In fact, she'd been trying out different poses in her room to see which one would look the most casual. After all, she didn't want her friends to think she *knew* she was a real genius! First she lay on her bed, feet crossed, and arms folded behind her head. That pose felt too relaxed, so she moved to the beanbag chair.

She waited there for a few minutes, expecting her friends to arrive momentarily. When they didn't come right away, she moved to her favorite spot and got into her favorite position: the middle of the floor, standing on her head. That was how her friends found her.

"How did you ever think of such a great idea as to send them each a valentine from each other?" Molly asked, tipping her head a little so she could get a better look at Stevie's face.

"We all found your notes this morning," Laura began to explain.

"And then Mrs. Hansen called Molly and said the same thing your note said," Meg continued.

"The wedding is on!" all three girls shrieked together. As they said it they hugged each other and hugged Stevie's feet, which were sticking straight up in the air.

"Eric got the valentine, which he thought was from Julie," Meg went on.

"And Julie got the valentine, which she thought was from Eric," Molly added, "and both of them forgave each other!"

"It's perfect again," Laura said in her dreamy way.

"And tonight is the rehearsal for the wedding, then the dinner at Cafe Roval. And Stevie, since you are the one who saved the whole thing you can't say you aren't coming. At least you have to come watch the rehearsal and have dinner with us." Molly was insistent.

Stevie didn't argue. "Yeah, sure, I'll come watch," she said. "And I'll even come to dinner, although nothing could make me eat any of that totally disgusting chocolate cake again!"

It was settled, then. Stevie would be a part of the group at least for the rehearsal and dinner. The girls spent the rest of the afternoon doing for Stevie what she had done for them. They judged how she looked in her party dresses and voted on the one they thought would look best for the dinner. They picked the same dress she had worn there the last time.

"At least this time I won't have to wear a wrist corsage that gives me a rash," Stevie said.

Mrs. Hansen agreed to drive the girls to the church and then to the restaurant afterward. They sang all the way, and even Stevie added her own harmonies when they sang an old song about going to the chapel to get married. At the church Julie and Eric were already standing at the altar practicing what they were to say the next day during the real wedding. The girls walked in just when the minister said, "And now you may kiss the bride."

When Stevie saw Eric lean down and kiss Julie

she almost wished she hadn't come to the rehearsal. Then Julie looked up at Eric with the happiest smile Stevie had ever seen.

"Isn't it so romantic?" breathed Laura, clutching her heart.

"Stevie!" called out Julie once she saw that she and the others had arrived. "And the rest of my junior bridesmaids, too! Terrific! Now we can run through the whole wedding so none of us makes a mistake tomorrow. Ready?"

"Ready!" said the three who were in the wedding.

Stevie and Mrs. Hansen sat quietly together and watched as the wedding procession started at the top of the aisle, led by the three junior bridesmaids. Stevie could see that it looked a little unbalanced with only three, but Meg tried to fill out the empty space by walking in the middle of the aisle. Behind Meg were the bridesmaids and ushers, and finally, Julie and her father. The rehearsal lasted for about forty-five minutes, with no one making any serious mistakes. When it was over, the bride and groom and the others went from the church to Cafe Roval.

When Stevie walked into the restaurant with her friends and Mrs. Hansen, she didn't feel nearly as uncomfortable as the first time she'd been there. She showed Meg, Molly, and Laura where to check their coats. She pointed out the napkins folded like swans and the butter molded in the same swan shape. She said, "Hi!" to the waiter who had unfolded her napkin for her, and he seemed to remember Stevie, too. Her friends stayed close to Stevie, because she seemed to know her way around this fancy place.

"Look at the silverware!" gasped Molly in a loud whisper.

"The little fork is a seafood fork," Stevie informed her friends wisely.

Stevie led the way through the dining room to another room that had been reserved for Julie's and Eric's dinner guests. Julie and Eric were already seated, as were their immediate family members, the bridesmaids, the ushers, and the best man. Eric stood up to show Mrs. Hansen to her seat, and the girls found their own place cards right opposite Julie.

The food was nothing like what Stevie had been served before. The salad had regular lettuce and lovely little tomatoes. The beef was delicious roast beef without the flaky pastry crust around it. The vegetables were fresh peas or corn, not a lima bean in sight. And the dessert was plain vanilla ice cream with a delicious hot fudge sauce drizzled lightly over it. Everything was as it should be, perfect. And at the end of the meal, Julie presented her bridesmaids with a gift. Each one received a gold bracelet with the wedding date engraved on it. And for each of the junior bridemaids there was another small box. Julie handed one to Meg, one to Molly, one to Laura, and one to Stevie.

"But I'm not in the wedding!" Stevie said, trying to give the box back to Julie.

"No, but you're in my heart." Julie smiled, pushing the box back to Stevie.

With tears in their eyes, the girls opened their boxes together and saw that they had each received a tiny gold locket with their names and the wedding date engraved on the back.

All the way home in Mrs. Hansen's car that night, the girls talked and talked about the wonderful night they had had with Julie. The excitement filled the air, and Mrs. Hansen sang along with the girls all the way home.

"See you tomorrow morning at the wedding!" she called out as she dropped each one off at her door. "I'll be there to help you all get dressed. Get a good night's sleep now."

All of them tried to sleep, but of course the excitement of the night and of the next day made it difficult to do more than just lie there in the dark listening to the clock ticking away the longest night they'd ever spent. At last, Valentine's Day and Julie's wedding day arrived.

Meg, Molly, and Laura had to be at the church early to get into their junior bridesmaids' dresses, pick up their bouquets of flowers, and have last-minute touches done to their hair. Stevie had planned to go later with her mother, but when she got up her mother said Mrs. Hansen was planning to pick her up and bring her to the church.

Stevie felt strange. The big day had finally arrived. She didn't feel angry or jealous anymore. In fact, she felt good that she had been the one to help Julie and Eric get over being mad with each other. But now, after all the times she had said, "Promise you won't try to change my mind," Stevie wished that someone, anyone, would try to change her mind. After all, this was the most important day of Julie's life, and Stevie did not want to be left out of that day.

A car horn honked out front.

"Stevie," called her mother from downstairs. "Mrs. Hansen is here."

"I'll be down in a minute!" called Stevie. She wasn't anywhere near ready. Quickly she pulled on a pair of jeans and a sweatshirt. Then she reached into her closet and tugged at a dress she didn't hate *too* much, threw it over her arm, picked up a pair of tights and party shoes, and left the drawer open with clothes hanging out of it. Habit made her pick up her Red Sox baseball cap and slap it on her head. "Coming!" she yelled again, hurrying to throw the spread up over her unmade bed. She ran down the stairs and out the door before her mother had a chance to see how she looked.

Mrs. Hansen couldn't help but laugh a little. "Oh, my Stevie!" she said when Stevie opened the door and got into the car. "That's quite an outfit you've got on to wear to a wedding. The hat really pulls it together."

Stevie reached up and felt her head. "Ohmigosh!" she said. "I was in such a rush I just grabbed my baseball hat and ran out! But I brought other stuff to change into." She pulled off her hat, revealing two scraggly braids.

"Oh, Stevie," sighed Mrs. Hansen with a smile. "What *are* we going to do with you?"

Stevie just laughed sheepishly. She didn't know the answer to that question.

Before she had time to think of an answer, Mrs. Hansen's car pulled into the parking lot of the church. "Hurry now, Stevie," Mrs. Hansen said. "We've got to get inside and get everyone ready. The girls will already be here, I think."

Stevie didn't move from her seat. She looked up and saw the church where Julie was going to be getting married. In a little more than one hour Julie McCarthy was going to be Mrs. Eric T. Bowen, and then she was going to be gone.

"Come along now, Stevie," Mrs. Hansen's voice called to her.

Stevie got out and walked inside with Mrs. Hansen. She could hear the giggles of the girls coming from the dressing room before Mrs. Hansen even opened the door. Stevie put on a brave face as she walked in.

"Oh! Thank goodness you're here!" Molly said breathlessly. "We thought you weren't going to make it! And Mrs. Hansen, we need your help with the pearl buttons and with our hair."

Mrs. Hansen laughed. "Oh, yes, I'll help you all. And you're all going to look just as pretty as can be." She helped each of the girls into their red velvet dresses and spent time buttoning the cuff buttons, straightening the hems, and adjusting the necklines. The girls giggled and wiggled with delight at each adjustment.

Stevie watched and helped by holding pins, tying ribbons, and doing the bending to buckle shoe straps. Amidst the happy noise of her friends, Stevie heard another voice coming from a connecting dressing room. In a moment, Julie appeared in the doorway looking like all the advertisements in the bridal magazines she'd shown them that first day at Mrs. Hansen's house.

"Julie!" gasped Stevie as her eyes beheld the most beautiful sight she had ever seen. Everything looked perfect, from the long white wedding gown, to the delicate floral headpiece, to the sweet-smelling bouquet of red and white baby roses.

"Well," said Julie, looking at her young friends, "it's almost time, and you all look beautiful."

Stevie saw herself in the mirror and knew that Julie couldn't possibly mean that she looked beautiful, too. She looked a mess, straggly reddish-blonde hair in two messy braids. Behind her own image she saw Molly, Meg, and Laura all dressed and ready to help Julie celebrate the most important day of her life.

"Are you absotively posolutely sure you won't change your mind, Stevie?" Julie said, meeting Stevie's eyes in the mirror.

Stevie looked back at Julie. "Well, I can't now," she said, "I don't even have a dress."

Julie smiled, and then Stevie saw why. Coming into the mirror was Mrs. Hansen's image, and she was holding up a red-velvet dress with pearls along the neckline and tiny pearl buttons at the cuffs. Stevie whirled around to see if the mirror was tricking her eyes. It wasn't. Mrs. Hansen really was standing there, and she really was holding a dress that looked to be exactly Stevie's size.

"Better hurry, Stevie," Mrs. Hansen said. "There isn't much time left now."

"And Stephanie Ames, *this* is the day we're going to do something to fix this hair of yours!" Julie put down her bouquet and began working on Stevie's hair. Meg, Molly, and Laura all helped Stevie unbutton the dress she was wearing and take it off. Then they helped her pull the dress Mrs. Hansen had made especially for her over her head. With her three best friends, her favorite "big sister," and Mrs. Hansen all working together to get her ready, Stevie felt as if she were caught in a car wash. But when they finished, she couldn't believe her eyes.

"Stevie Ames, I knew it could be done! You look beautiful! Stunning! Gorgeous!" Julie said, standing next to Stevie and proudly admiring her.

Stevie looked at the two of them standing there together. Her hair hung down smooth and shiny, just like Julie's. Her blue eyes sparkled, just like Julie's. And across her nose and cheeks her freckles dotted her face, just like Julie's.

"Sisters, right?" Julie said, seeing all the same things Stevie was seeing.

"Sisters," said Stevie softly.

Strains of organ music drifted into the dressing room, causing a whole new flurry of excitement. Julie kissed her junior bridesmaids, all *four* of them, and gracefully went out the door. "Wish me luck," she said before she left.

"Good luck!" they all said together.

"Good luck," Stevie wished again. And this was *one* wish Stevie really hoped would come true.

When Meg's kooky aunt and unusual neighbor give her a makeover, will her life ever be the same? Read Friends 4-Ever #11, BEST WISHES, WHOEVER YOU ARE.